TABLE OF CONTENTS

1 A FEW WHOM I HAVE MET 1
2 TRUMPETS DO BLOW 5
3 DON'T JEST WITH A JESTER 29
4 MATCHMAKER 37
5 THE STASH 63
6 THE CASE OF THE CUDDLING CAT 95
7 GET OFF MY BED 115
8 DISAPPEARING GOLF BALLS 139
9 DOWN BY THE RIVERSIDE 175
10 EMERALDS FROM THE ISLE 203
ACKNOWLEDGMENTS 223

1   A FEW WHOM I HAVE MET

I DIDN'T MEAN TO. They just started visiting me. It happened early on in my life, and not understanding who they were and why they were there, I put them down to a figment of my imagination and we got along great. Many children do that until they make the mistake of mentioning their imaginary friends to their parents. As the firstborn and only son in a family where expectations were high for my future, I kept my playmates' existence to myself. We played together when I was lonely. They always let me win at board games and races in the backyard. Every so often, if my mother heard me laughing at nothing at all, she would shoot me a "Did you see one, Danny?" look.

I grew to ignore her, as I didn't want to be associated with the *I see dead people* cult. Why was this happening? I should have asked when I had the chance.

As I grew older, I grew weary of them pouncing into my space sometimes at the most inopportune times. How could I relax and dream about the girl I met in Chemistry 101 when there would be apparitions intruding and wanting to give me unsolicited advice on how to win her over in exchange for a favour? How that bothered me. I turned my back to them and ignored them. Somehow, I was able to forget all about them for a few years.

Until they came back! I expect it was because I was a softie and gave in to a few old souls from the other realm who seemed harmless and in need of help. They were sworn to keep me a secret. I didn't want to be inundated with silly requests and ceaseless jabber. They didn't listen, though, or keep their promise. They faded right back from whence they came and bragged about their success in settling old scores. "This young man was a great help; we recommend his services," they would say. Enjoying my downtime started to become difficult, as it was apparent that there was a lineup of departed souls with a final wish from their earthly time that had not been fulfilled. I never knew when they would bounce forth or what demand they would make. They usually took pleasure in disturbing my relaxation. *Time out*, I would think, catch an even breath, and then before you could say, "Holy Ghost," one or maybe two would appear: some silly, some angry, some quite fretful.

I soon developed a barrier system that has worked to keep them at bay most of the time, but not always. So, feeling the need to take matters into my own hands, I have captured some tales of those who snuck through my aura on my computer and a backup hard drive.

At times, there is no pleasure in their dealings. You see, out there, in the realm of who knows where, you are either a ghost or a spirit, and these two groups are quite different in their makeup and their requests. I figure they are placed into one of two categories depending on how they had conducted their time on Earth. Don't ask me the ins and outs of that—it is just what I've observed over time.

The spirits are the most demanding. They can be arrogant and mean. They expect instant gratification or are wont to throw things at or around me. They have a stronger power to exercise their desires than ghosts do, and they can retain their ability for a longer time. They are, however, confined to the area where they gave up their human identity. It might vary for a kilometre or two, depending on the situation, but sometimes, they are restricted to just a few metres and that can make them quite angry. I shut those down as fast as I can and refuse to deal with them.

The ghosts are quite the opposite. They are, for the most part, friendly, polite, and grateful for any help I can give them. They have limited power. They are not able to influence any earthly object or person by moving or touching them. They can move about freely anywhere they wish, but that takes a good deal of their limited energy, so they must be careful of their usage. If their energy is used, then *poof*! Away they go!

Both ghosts and spirits are shrouded in a cold atmosphere. A spirit's air tends to be somewhat acrid. I can usually fend them off by taking the Lord's name in vain. It appears they feel a burn from blasphemy.

I'm not sure why they pick on me or how they find me. Could it be they recognize the weak link in my aura? Why do I have this weak link? I don't know, nor do I know who to ask now that Mother is gone. Like most young people, it never occurred to me to ask her about our family history or why I suffer in this way. I suspect she did too, but the subject was never broached.

There have been times I've asked a kindly ghost if they have met my mother or if they have knowledge about the part of my family history that has left me with this problem. So far, none have admitted to catching sight of her, telling me that she must have led a satisfactory life and was able to pass right on through to everlasting glory. Way to go, Mom!

I have made it known among my ghost and spirit clientele that no violence must have occurred during their passing and that monetary payment is not an option. I thought this would discourage them, as I assumed it would be difficult for them to find a way to deliver any sort of compensation, but it didn't. I also advised them extra money in my coffers would not work, as I would have no way to hide it from the outstretched hand of the revenue department that works diligently across our land.

At times, the payment is enriching, other times... not so much. For better or for worse, it was the curiosity about their requests that led me to take up the occupation of Detective Daniel O'Patrick—first class, I might add—and go to work in Toronto, Ontario, for the CODA (Central Ontario Detective Agency), eking out an interesting living.

2 TRUMPETS DO BLOW

DURING MY OFF-HOURS, I love to amble through the mazes offered up in antique shops and musty barns alive with old life. Toronto has many shops, but they are, for the most part, neat and refined. When you go out of the city, you find wonderful buildings to explore.

So it was, one Friday morning, heading north to my cottage, I stopped at an old barn that was advertising antiques and collectibles, instead of cows. It was sitting high upon a hill, near the village of Washago. The sign on the highway advised you to "enter here" and "exit there." With instructions so exact, one has to do what one is told, right?

I don't know why I purchased the trumpet; I don't play. It wasn't even the trumpet I first noticed. It was the customer holding it and giving it a disdainful once-over. He was pushing on the second valve and proclaiming it to be sticky and probably corroded. Loud derogatory statements by patrons of this kind are given as a signal to the proprietor that "your price is too high, but I am willing to negotiate." He unceremoniously dropped the trumpet down from whence he found it and carried on along the earthen aisle. Sliding right in behind him, I picked up the abused item and cradled it in both hands. I know not why, other than I thought it deserved better treatment than it had just been given. Unfortunately, I am not a man that is blessed with the gift of making music, but I do appreciate hearing the sounds made by those who are.

The trumpet was old; there was no doubting that. When I tipped it up on its end, engraving could be seen running downward toward the bell. It was brass and in dire need of a cleaning. There was some script on it, but all that could be made out was "*pat. pen Ohio Band*" and what appeared to be a crown. How does one clean a brass trumpet? This one would need some scrubbing.

I pushed the second valve down and it stayed down instead of popping back up as I believe is expected once one takes one's finger off. On the front of the slide, I noticed a latch. When I attempted to push on it, it was reluctant to move. I could detect a small hole underneath. Later, I was to learn this small latch was a water key and had a very important function on a trumpet. I knew nothing about trumpets, only my love of hearing them in a band or on their own—Louis Armstrong, notwithstanding, or Kaempfert's sexy rendition of "Wonderland by Night." Who, tell me, is not moved by the personal stories told by "Taps" or a solo trumpeter giving his all to "Amazing Grace"?

There was a small yellow tag knotted to a ring by a rather dirty white string. This was an indication that the trumpet had been sitting on the top of that old bureau for some time, along with many other misfits. The price to me did not seem out of line and required no loud indignation for the benefit of the storeowner. Under the price of thirty-five dollars was inked in red "15% off." That would pay for the tax.

Decision made, I wandered forth to the beautiful antique cash register that was still in use. As I laid my unjustified purchase on the long bar counter, the mouthpiece fell off. The preceding customer looked back at me and jeered, "Another piece broke on it. You did notice the broken valve, right?"

Before I could respond, the owner informed us the mouthpiece is supposed to come off for cleaning and replacement if needed. He scrutinized the mouthpiece in question and informed us it was round and probably not the original. "This trumpet would be from the thirties," he added—another piece of information applied to the bottom rung of my learning curve.

I let the trumpet be a passenger on the front seat of my SUV. It lay there quite contented as I barrelled north along Highway 11. I tuned my radio to the local golden-oldies station, just in time to catch Louie tuning up for his trumpet solo of "A Kiss to Build a Dream On". With my new/old trumpet so close beside me, I imagined it was blasting out those high C notes. What a trip I was having, speeding along, singing along, and going down memory lane.

It was dusk when I reached my lakeside retreat. Fall is a peaceful time on my lake. The sun was setting leaving a trail of rippling gold as its goodbye. A loon's call echoed as the bullfrogs' chorus filled the air. I grabbed my overnighter from the back seat, my laptop case and trumpet from the front seat, and headed inside, ready to hunker down for the weekend and finish up notes on my last agency assignment.

All was well as I ran through the usual cottage chores. I opened blinds and windows, checked the lights and plumbing, and finally settled down with a local Muskoka ale while I prepared dinner purchased along the way.

The first deep relaxed breath I caught as I sank back into my easy bean bag brought her forth. This ghostly apparition,

I must admit, caught me very much by surprise. I was out of my reasoning and comfort zone with this one.

She was beautiful. She stood directly in front of me, slightly bent forward, hands on hips, and elbows pointing outward. She was the colour of dark chocolate, tall, and slim, her long legs showing below a silk dress that stopped slightly below her knees. Her shoes had Cuban heels. I suppose I kept my attention on those shoes for a while, as I was hesitant to raise my gaze once more above those knees. I looked up slowly, taking in a dress sporting large red flowers of a non-descript kind on a navy blue background. It sat on her hips quite tightly; her hands seemed to be holding it there. The neckline plunged much too low for any self-respecting ghost. From her ears dangled long earrings with a cluster of red cherries made from Bakelite plastic—quite sought-after in today's collectible market. Her shiny black hair was swept up at the back and sat in sausage-sized ringlets on top of her head, kept in place with hairpins. Her lips and cheek rouge were as red as the dangling cherries. Black eyebrows and deep brown eyes gave me a look that radiated trouble times ahead with this one. The only thing modern about this ghostly wisp was attitude.

I stared. I waited. She spoke.

"Close your mouth, white boy. You're droolin.'"

I did. I closed my mouth, blinked my eyes, took a slug of my ale, and knew it would be a struggle to maintain control.

I began our introduction as politely as I could. I was confident she was a ghost and not a spirit, as she was here invading my territory and I was relatively certain she did not meet her demise on my lakefront. I cleared my throat. "I suppose you have come about my trumpet." That was as far as I got before she abruptly interrupted me in a somewhat sarcastic way.

"No, honey, it's about MY trumpet!"

"I just paid thirty-five dollars for it, including tax. It may have been yours once, but now it's mine . . . honey." One would think by now I would have learned not to argue or be a smart mouth with apparitions, as it is a losing game, but this one tempted me big time.

"I have been led to believe by acquaintances of mine that you hold no stock in monetary payments, so thirty-five Canadian dollars has little value. That trumpet, y'all hear me, was given special to me. No other like it."

It was beside me on the table. I reached for it, held it tight, and looked it over as if I knew what I was looking for. Fooling this lovely Southern mint julep, I'm sure I was not. "You mean, it's a one-off?"

"A one what?" She moved a little closer, too close for comfort actually. The cold air wafted with a thick smell of magnolia perfume. "If y'all mean is there just one like it, y'all is right."

She held out her hands and wiggled all ten of her fingers in the direction of my trumpet. Each digit ended in glittering cherry-red polish. "Oh, I'd give the devil his due to hold it and blow some."

"Blasphemy!" I shouted. I pulled my trumpet back out of harm's way. "You're not playing fair with a statement like that. You know the rules, or you wouldn't be here."

"Fo!" She blew me off with a downward flip of her fingers. "You Northern folk still is so uptight. I see Canadians is no better than Yankees. Simmer down, honey; turn it over for me now. See the dent on the lip of the bell?"

It was not difficult to identify the dent on the bell rim. The damage on the turn itself was slight, but under that there was an inward dent about four centimetres in length. The years of mould and neglect had hidden the damage.

She moved around it as best she could, bending her lovely head this way and that. It was obvious she would indeed give the devil his due if she could pick it up, but ghostly hands would slide right through like the proverbial hot knife on butter.

"Someone along the way has given it a new mouthpiece."

"How can you tell that?"

"'Cause, *chéri*, I kept the original."

Question not the wisdom of a ghost. I knew all in good time she would get me to where she wanted me to be. I tried to change the direction of the path she was bent on taking me down.

"It's been a few years, I surmise." I tried so hard to sound knowledgeable. "It looks like it has had some rough treatment."

"No, honey, I caused that damage myself when I threw it at my no-good, nigga' husband."

I must admit, that shook me up. I was still sitting, and she was standing. That gave her the advantage of superiority, so I set the trumpet on the end table and stood.

"How do I know this was yours? Why would you keep just the mouthpiece? Just because you threw it at your African-American husband, doesn't mean it was yours."

"My what?" She looked querulously at me. It appeared she was as offended with my interpretation of her dearly departed as I was with hers.

We stared. My, she was extremely beautiful. It was not for me to wonder or query what her life was, or how she met her end at such a young age; it was for me to get on with it.

"I need to ascertain it was yours and what you want me to do and what will be your payment."

She settled quickly into the business at hand. There sat my drink and instant dinner, wasting away and quickly becoming fodder for the recycle bin.

"You named it a 'one-off.' No other like it—that's right, sweet man. Somewheres in the middle of 1930, it was. A salesman from Ohio came down to New Orl'ns."

"Down to where?" I was stupid to interrupt.

"New Orl'ns. I will just say this once for your Northern ears, so mind me now. *NEW. OR. LEANS!*"

"Carry on," I proclaimed cheerily, trying to sound more British than Canadian. I don't think she cared.

"His company was making changes to their line of band instruments in Cleveland. Once y'all get my trumpet cleaned up, you will see the etching of a crown—the Regent Ohio—and "Patent Pending. #901." The only trumpet with that mark, my love, as it was the first and the only one. The company wasn't sure about the sound with the brass or the bell size. The man needed to hear the trumpet with true jazz. You couldn't find that sound in Ohio. Where do you go? To New Orl'ns, of course. I knowed he had no intention of giving this trumpet to me, but circumstances led him to leave it in my hotel room. Don't give me any of your looks of bad ideas now. Hear me out." She added the last sentence quickly, with her hands waving palms upward in my direction as if to hush me before I could pass judgment.

"I could play a mean horn in my day. All in the business knew so and said so. All in the business also didn't like to let a woman play with a band and said so. They was so afraid they would be outshone by a woman. That's how insecure some of thems were. They just wanted a woman's body and voice out in front of the boys in the band. I schemed to do both and I did. Not sorry, no, I'm not."

She shook her beautiful head negatively, which agreed with her last statement, and those bright cherry earrings swung keeping time. "That Ohio man came into the club one afternoon when the boys were gone. He told me his story 'bout needing to hear a New Orl'ns sound coming through. He took that very one, right there, out of its case and handed it to me. *Chéri*, I knew I could blow a New Orl'ns sound like he never had heard before. Next, I lied just a little, but the good Lord, He forgave me. Truth, I said, 'My husband, he plays trumpet in this famous New Orl'ns jazz club, and I sing here. Bring it up to my room and leave it with me, sir. I will see that he gets it tonight. You can stay and hear the sound.' My mistake was bringing this white man to my room, but I didn't want anyone coming in the club and seeing me playing trumpet for him."

She turned from me and gazed out the window, taking in the view of the lake. "Nice place y'all got here."

"Stop with the stall." I almost added the word "Moll" to be in keeping with the decade but held it back in time.

She folded her arms and paced the floor. "He came up to my room willing enough, closed the door, and handed me the case." She flipped one hand over in the direction of my trumpet. "I took that beauty out and smoothed it over.

"That mouthpiece just fit so right, baby. I blasted out the scale of B-flat in perfection, and that man knew he was hearing New Orl'ns sound. Others in those upstairs rooms heard that sound too. That's where the band slept in the daytime, and here, I had woken some. There was a poundin' and a yellin' at the door for Henry—he was my man—to take it downstairs. Now let me tell you, this Ohio man was whiter than a beginner's ghost-white. I think he pictured his fate at being caught in my room if Henry should appear.

"'Wait just one minute,' I advised him. 'They will be gone; then you can make your way down and out.' He nodded, waited, then vanished, leaving behind my trumpet."

"Fascinating story," I conceded. "But not proof of past ownership and why you threw it at husband Henry."

She stopped pacing and leaned against the far wall. I could tell from past experiences that she was running out of ghostly energy. I did wish she would hurry, as being left in the middle of a muddle was very exasperating on my part.

"Look there." She indicated with a wave of her hand that I should pick up the trumpet. "Just on the mouthpiece receiver."

That I could find, thanks to the storekeeper's lesson.

"What do you see there, honey?"

"Some zigzag lines."

"Oh my Lord!" She twirled about with the back of one hand on her forehead. "They ain't making 'em any smarter these days! Look again. Initials: M. W. And that don't mean Mae West!"

I looked. When will I ever learn!

"My initials, for Masie Wesson. I scratched them on after that Ohio man skedaddled out of my room and booted it right back to his safe part of town.

"That evening, I was prime for my singing time with the band, but I had a surprise in store for them. Never had those men bosses given a lady a chance to try out with a trumpet, so I was about to bring a tryout to them. The band warmed up; playing real good, they was. I was singing and gyrating my moving parts to the appreciation of all patrons. Near the end of the set, the band broke into 'And the Angels Sing.' I sang the first stanza, then reached down and picked up my trumpet and blasted out my whole self into perfect sound. My whole body, honey, just went with it. Damn hot degrees, it was. Just eight decades ahead of my time, that's all. I stopped, so sure they would have to agree I was *dy-na-mite!*"

She looked so sad, as her memory conjured up a bad time.

"The club was heavy with silence. The cigar smoke swirling through the crowd appeared to be the only motion. I looked out at all them men sitting there. I couldn't tell what they was thinking. Next thing I knowed, Henry was pulling and yanking me and my trumpet stage left. Up the stairs, he dragged me, into our room. He threw me with such a force that I hit the floor sliding but managed to hang on to my trumpet. I got to my feet fast 'cause Henry was coming at me. 'Damn girl, whatcha think you was doin'? No one was 'pectin' you to mess us up like that!'

"I backed up as far as I could and let fly with that trumpet. And, sweetheart, that is the cause of the dent on the rim and the need for a new mouthpiece."

"Whew!" I felt as exhausted as she looked. "And?"

"That was the cause of the dent on Henry's head too. He put his hand up on top and it come away with his blood. I was sure I was in for a slapping 'round good, but the bangin' on the door told me some of the other men from the band had come right on up after him. Henry deviled me with a 'I get you next time, girl' stare, reached down, and snatched up my trumpet. Marched out with a slam. I never did see him or my trumpet again. The mouthpiece had fallen off when it bounced off Henry's head to the floor. There it was for me to keep. A short time after all was said and done, I etched my initials M. W. on the tip of it too."

"So, where is it now?"

"I don't know, *chéri*. I kept it safe with me all my time on Earth. I'd hoped my daughter would keep it too, but I think the family lost track of such a tiny thing that had no meaning for them. That's how it goes with the mementoes of the dearly departed.

"When you get to New Orl'ns for Mardi Gras, you go find my daughter's chil', *mon arrière petit fille*. I suspect she plays a mean trumpet just like I did. These days, she can. Life's some easier for our babies than it was for us. If she practise and works hard, she can do what I surely wish I could have. Not that I want her to live my life. No, siree!"

"I'm not going to Mardi Gras. That's in the spring, isn't it? Never been there, not of interest. Job declined, Miss Masie."

She sauntered close to me. I think she knew I hated that.

"You, *mon chéri*, your future. You'll be in New Orl'ns for Mardi Gras. From now till that time, find a real good trumpet repairman to fix and clean my trumpet. Tell him to leave the bell dent. Get a case for it. When y'all find my baby, she'll be a real beauty of a young lady by now I 'spect. Give her my trumpet. Let her know her *arrière grand-mère* was the only one to blow through on that trumpet with its original mouthpiece. Now, how special is that! Your payment will be a private performance for y'all by a well-known exceptional trumpet player. He'll knock your socks off, baby, and leave you dumbfounded. Y'all will find this a full payment when you hear his notes."

Then she faded away, leaving me in the dark both literally and figuratively.

It didn't take me long to realize thirty-five dollars was just a down payment on this trumpet. The repairman was mystified by my request to fix it but leave the dent. An explanation was not offered.

A look into my future came as a CODA assignment. The agency hired me out as detail for security in New Orleans for three weeks during Mardi Gras. From my prep reading, I learned New Orleans is a city with a rich history of ghosts, spirits, and conjurers. How will I ever get some downtime? Will I have a target on my weak aura? Masie, my guiding ghost, never appeared again to give me courage, instructions, or clues.

Nevertheless, off I flew with a trumpet case as my carry-on. If I lost it as checked luggage, I knew I would be doomed with visions of ghostly Masies forever.

I was billeted in apartments with many other security guards and given my hours and locations on arrival, and the whirlwind began.

If you have never been to Mardi Gras, you must put it on your bucket list. It swallows you up in the moves and din. You become one with the whole. The music will claim you, and you will find yourself rejoicing, singing, and dancing along with strangers who are fluid motion shoulder to hip with you and have suddenly become your friends. That is where my duties began for the public's safety. Difficult as it was, I found I was able to keep a clear head and mind and watch out for the evildoers among the crowds. The French Quarter was the best and the worst.

During my free time, with a tourist map in hand, I roamed at will, hypnotized by the architecture, sounds, smells, and glorious food that was so enticing. Jackson Square and the Pontalba Buildings were familiar to me only from pictures, so I needed to investigate.

I had so little to go on in the search for Masie's *arrière petit fille*. She would be in her thirties, perhaps, she would be musical, perhaps, and she would live in New Orleans, perhaps. I had checked out many of the hot-spot nightclubs that hosted live music. Many sported photos of days gone by, and while they were nostalgic, they gave me little information. Most were of Black musicians, some with a female singer at the mic, but none came close to looking like my beautiful Masie or gave me a clue as to what I might be looking for.

I watched the marching parades whether I was on duty or not. Some were women brass bands dressed in wonderful costumes. There were Baby Doll Ladies in the St. Charles procession, the NOLA Chorus Flapper Girls and the Jewels from the jazz age. They were all tall, young, and beautiful.

I considered visiting some of the many museums in this magnificent city but knew enough to steer clear of the Museum of Death, the History of Voodoo Museum, the Haunted Museum, and all cemeteries. My weak aura would never be able to hold back a flood of unwanted guests.

My three-week stay was drawing quickly to a close, and as enjoyable as it was, I was making no headway in finding Masie's great-granddaughter. Sprawled out on a cast-iron bench in Louis Armstrong Park, gazing at his larger-than-life statue, and holding his larger-than-life trumpet, I held a solo pity party. I would have to confess to Masie I was a complete New Orleans failure or she would have to dig up some more bones for me.

"Come on, Louie," I called out. I knew by now it was quite sane to yell, sing, dance, or do whatever moved you in public during this *"laissez les bon temps rouler"* in New Orleans. "Blast me out 'Let's Call the Whole Thing Off'!"

I sank back, head down, legs akimbo and relaxed. A cold wind chilled the right side of me.

"Masie?" How hopeful I was.

I turned my head, only to be confronted with a jester. He mimicked my ungainly sitting style, with his head turned toward me. His harlequin costume flashed in the Mardi Gras colours of teal, purple, and yellow. Ruffles adorned his neck, wrists, and ankles. His head displayed a tri-pointed cap. His face was covered with a white mask, except for his bearded chin. White runners covered his feet, and mega beads dangled from his wrists. His straggly beard and bare hands told me this was a white jester. His smile was not engaging.

I waited. He spoke.

"Oh, sorry. I sense you have a client." He gathered his presence and was in the process of a disappearing act as he sauntered away.

My reaction took over. "Wait!" I shouted as I sat up straight. "Maybe you can help me."

He turned around, stood still, and became a brighter image. "Help you? You have that backwards, don't you, bro? I was about to ask for your help; then I am beholden to give you a favour." He paused and spun around on his sneakered toes to turn back and face me, all the while juggling four balls of Mardi Gras colours with all his beads clicking. "But, this could be an interesting switch. I help y'all, and the beholden is to me."

Through his mask, I detected eyes that held the calculations of a devious mind. He twirled once more and came back around sans the balls. I needed balls.

"Are you a ghost or a spirit?" I asked, feeling as though I should have been asking if he was a good witch or a bad witch, as I knew I was not in Canada anymore.

"I am a spirit," he answered promptly and rather proudly. "Now, how can I help y'all?"

Spirits, with practise, have the strength to move objects but not the ability to move too far away from the area of their demise, therefore I deduced, Jester must stay within the confines of New Orleans and I would be leaving in two days.

"What payment will you want?"

"Not sure yet. I need to think on it. Depends on the help y'all require. So, tell me." He leaned forward and stroked his scraggly beard in a manner of conniving interest.

Spirits are gifted with more energy than ghosts. I suppose it may be because they are not moving too far afield, so I knew I would have more talking time with him than I did with Masie. He twirled his beads and twinkled on his toes as I related my whole megillah in finding Masie's *arrière petit fille*.

From the commencement of my tale to its closing, only a few strollers in the park glanced my way. In this year of our Lord, many of us talk into an earpiece and no one cares.

Jester staged an elaborate bow—one foot forward, one hand flouncing—and gave me his response.

"What a fortunate fellow you are. Entertainers in the Big Easy gather together during the year whenever possible. As it happens, my friend, I know of a Masie that blows a mean trumpet. It may not be your Masie's Masie, but it might be worth your time to run her down—figuratively, I mean, not literally." He shuddered when he realized the words he had spoken. Too close to his own fate, perhaps.

"The sweet Masie of my acquaintance lives southeast of New Orleans in Old Aurora, but comes in to play with the band called Trumpettes of the Jazz Age. They wear shimmy dresses of the Mardi Gras colours, with fluffy-feather high caps. They dance the Charleston and Black Bottom as they move on down the line. Bessie Smith would be so proud of them. Now I do believe the last parade, Krewe of Pontchartrain, is tomorrow. It starts at one o'clock at the corner of Napoleon and Tehoupitoulas and ends at Poydras Street. The Masie of my former acquaintance is tall and curvy and has a full-blown Afro parted down the middle. I'll check back at cha' later, bro."

And poof! He was gone.

Be it luck or destiny, it matters little. My last duty was to mingle in the crowd for the Pontchartrain Parade, so I was stationed at the corner a good two hours before start time. Suddenly, a bevy of lovely young ladies arrived from all directions. They were all carrying trumpets and were all in identical glitter and wearing high fluffy-feathered caps pulled tightly down upon their heads. No full Afro had a snowball's chance in hell to escape that headgear. Fully bewildered, I was. Had Jester joked me? I was on duty, so I couldn't do much but follow along with the march weaving through the crowd, keeping my eyes everywhere but on the parade.

It seemed to take forever to reach the end. As each marching group reached their debarkation area, they dispersed with practiced turns. The Trumpettes of the Jazz Age seemed to meld as one to the side as they waited for their ride back to their staging area.

I shouldered my way into the middle of the group, ignoring the looks and elbows. In an attempt to appear as if I belonged, I began to shout ever so lovingly, "Masie? Masie?"

The young ladies were starting to take off their headdresses, and I was milling around in circular directions, still shrilling out her name. None so far had a full-blown Afro. I was starting to get dagger looks, and fears of a female ambush were beginning to set in.

"Do I know you?" a sweet mellow voice behind me sounded, like a blessing.

I elbowed my way around and bumped unceremoniously into a Masie that could have been my Masie but much more grounded. She backed up and looked down at me. I am not short, but she was not either and her advantage was high heels. How they ever walked and danced all that way on those platforms is still a mystery to me.

She reached up to her headdress, removed a few hairpins with practiced style, and pulled off the feathers. Up popped a full-blown Afro parted straight down the middle.

"No, Masie, you don't know me. I am Detective Dan O'Patrick from Canada, on security duty here, but I have done some work on your behalf before I got here and have located something that belongs to your family."

All this was said quickly and streamlined as we were jostled back and forth by members of the band and other marchers. Masie was called to jump on the back of a float if she wanted to get back to her area.

"Follow our float!" she yelled at me.

"I don't have a car."

"Then come with us."

She grabbed my hand and yanked me along with her. Up onto the float with her band, I went. Rather fun, it was.

It was early evening when I was finally off duty and able to meet up with Masie at a café of her choosing. I took the trumpet in its new case with me, as during the float ride, I had barged ahead and asked her if by chance she had a trumpet mouthpiece. She was startled by my forwardness and questioned me but verified she did. She further verified there were M. W. initials on it. She loved that, as her name was Masie Wellington. Quite a coincidence, she thought. She knew nothing more about it, though.

I presented Masie with the trumpet, case and all. I told her about her *arrière grand-mere*, including the story of how the dent on the bell got there. I embellished somewhat. Every good family story needs embellishment, don't you think? Masie was in emotional tears when I ended my story. She asked how I knew about this.

"I'm a detective; I detect," is always my go-to response.

I had but one day left in New Orleans before my flight north. It had been a most enjoyable assignment—a combination of work, play, and a new culture I will not elaborate upon, except to let you know I will enjoy gumbo and jambalaya with fond memories but never order grits with my breakfast.

I would wait now with anticipation for my payment from Masie, but I was very uneasy in the Big Easy about my pact with Jester. I knew I had crossed the line with my reversed role. Not only that, but I had done so not knowing his required payment. A promise made is a debt unpaid, and to leave a pact unfinished in the realm of the unknown can lead to dire consequences.

I missed my trumpet but knew it was where it rightfully belonged. I decided to take a walk along Esplanade Ave. to visit the Jazz Museum and the Old Mint. That would make a fond farewell to my three weeks in the deep south. I found it without trouble. An old insignificant-looking building, it was. There did not appear to be much activity around it. Perhaps with Mardi Gras and all that real jazz, it held little interest.

I approached the door and tried the latch. Nothing moved. An attached notice indicated I was within the opening hours. Not to be undaunted, I tried the latch again with more force. I shook it; I rattled it. That got the attention of an inside attendant.

She hurried to the door. I could see through the thick glass, she was somewhat annoyed at the incessant rattling and banging I was creating, but true to the genteel nature of a Southern belle, as she opened the door, she smiled and informed me, "Sweetheart, we have closed today, as we have allowed a special guest to use our facilities to prepare for an honour he has been given."

"But," I insisted, "I have come all the way from Canada"—I play that card for all it is worth, 'cause Americans think we are all really nice, eh!—" to spend a little time here before I return home tomorrow morning."

"I'm so sorry, honey, truly I am."

"Let him in, Laurie Ann. An audience of one will do no harm," the voice behind her echoed down the hall.

Still guarding the door like a goalie, she turned her head and asked with kind respect, "Are you sure, sir? We did promise you your solitude."

"I'm sure, Laurie Ann." He came closer to the door and addressed me. "Welcome to our city. Come in. Follow me if you will."

Laurie Ann graciously stepped aside and allowed me entry. I bowed my head in a thank-you to her, as somehow I had the feeling I was privileged.

I fell in behind him as we walked down a dark hallway and into a rotunda with a rather high ceiling. There was little in the room except for a few square glass exhibit cases. He had a trumpet in his right hand that he swung loosely in time with his steps. When he came to the centre of the room, he stopped and turned to face me. Did the astonished look on my naive Canadian face give me away?

"You're... you're..." I pointed my finger and accused him.

"Indeed I am, sir. Pleased to make your acquaintance. I have a solo performance coming up for our president. I find the acoustics in this room the best for attuning my sounds to what I am trying to achieve. I heard from your words at the door that you are a visitor to the USA. Once more, welcome. Find yourself a comfortable spot and tell me what you would like to hear."

I looked around, which wasn't difficult in an empty room, and settled for an area on the floor facing him. I sat with my back to the wall and my knees up, wrapping my arms around them.

"I love a trumpet, even though I can't play," I blathered forth. "You, in my opinion, are second only to Louie Armstrong himself."

He chuckled with his chin down as he is prone to do. "Thank you. A great compliment. If you had said better than Louie, I would have known you were pole fishing. I did, I will tell you, meet Louis when I was a little boy. I was not very old, but I remember him clearly. He spoke to me and encouraged me to pursue my interest in music if that is what I wanted and give no notice to the critics or naysayers but always be ready to accept valid corrections and criticism. So, what would you like to hear?"

Without thinking, as I am prone to do, I answered quickly, "'Amazing Grace.'"

"Everyone's favourite." His answer reeked of disappointment. As he raised the fine brass to his lips, ready to intake, again, I blurted out. "No, make it 'Just a Closer Walk With Thee.'"

With both hands, he projected his trumpet forward in my direction and softly said, "Much better."

If you have ever been fortunate to know the experience of having your soul take flight and the world no longer existing, you will understand what I am aiming to express. Each slow pure note he pushed through his horn was perfection unto itself. My head fell to my knees. The sound reached my ears and reverberated down to the very core of my being. All was forgiven, making me pure and transformed. I hung on to each note reluctant to give it up as the next one slowly took its place. Time had no meaning. There was no time. The moment was infinite. My meaning was fulfilled.

I am not sure I knew when the trumpet stopped and I became aware of the silence. I looked up, knowing my face was wet with flowing tears. I made no effort to wipe them away.

He bent forward slightly, arms straight at his sides, trumpet held as a sacred symbol. He spoke softly. "Take all the time you need, sir. I will wait outside. I am humbled by your graciousness." He turned and left the rotunda.

I did wait. I am not sure how long. I needed to recuperate from my overwhelming response to his gift. It finally dawned on me: my waiting was taking his time. I rose and slowly walked out, down the hall, through the door, into the sunshine. I stood there a moment to gather myself. The breeze was soft and fresh as its murmur trickled through the trees. A bird or two called and a far-off horn of a riverboat lamented. Reality returned as a car horn blasted through. I walked back up the avenue, cleansed and exhausted.

I returned to my hotel room and flopped face down on the bed, thinking a short nap wouldn't hurt before I packed up and headed out to the Louis Armstrong Airport. I was entertaining the thought of squelching on my deal with Jester. If I could sneak out of New Orleans without him squeezing in through my weak link, I would be home free. But could I live with myself if I was a cheat? Well, I could try.

I had to hold that thought as cold air wafted around me. I was surprised to recognize the tantalizing aroma of Masie perfume but, at the same time, relieved Jester had not pounced upon me so soon. I sat up to find her circling the room, giving it a full inspection. With her hands on her hips, in the pose she presented when I had first met her, she seemed to have more interest in the surroundings than in me.

"Looking for something?" I inquired.

Still on the hunt and ignoring me, she answered, "Changes have been made. You got your own closet with a sink, toilet, and bathtub shower. My Lord! Now ain't you the privileged one!"

"Not really, Masie. While I am happy to see you, I was expecting you later at my lake."

"I can travel, you know, honey, but it drains my power. I'm guessing I won't need it anymore, right?"

"Yes, your great-granddaughter did have the mouthpiece and now she has the trumpet. All is well."

I waited. She knew I was, and she let me. Finally, she turned, with those cherry red earrings still swinging.

"Was your private trumpet solo performance payment in full, chéri?"

"More than enough, Masie; much more than I ever could have imagined. I was blown away."

She smiled, and with her hands still on her hips, she swayed just a little to be provocative. Looking over my head at nothing in particular and breathing in a dream-like state, she whispered, "Second only to Louie himself."

Where had I heard that before? I suspected Masie was getting around more than mere mortals knew.

I was afraid she was about to make her grand exit, and I did want her to linger just a little longer. "Did you know," I rushed forth, "he met Louie when he was a young lad?"

Masie then looked directly at me in that secret annoying way that ghosts have that translates as "I know something you don't."

"Honey chil'," she purred. "I'm truly happy for him, but..." She hesitated as if considering her confession. She turned her head and wistfully continued, "I knew Louie when he was a young man." Slowly and dreamily, Masie faded away into the everlasting, leaving me with a wonder and a fantasy.

3 DON'T JEST WITH A JESTER

I WAS FEELING A melancholy satisfaction after the Masie apparition sprinkled away. I caught a short nap followed by a lunch of garlic shrimp and hush puppies. I had time to contemplate my packed bag and unworthy intentions of flying the coop and leaving unfinished business with Jester. My conscious stamped a pang of guilt warning on me. I relented, knowing this would be an unCanadian thing to do in the land of our big brother. Besides, who knew what punishment may lurk on the fuzzy side waiting for me? So, I steeled myself for an impending visit from Jester.

I didn't know what to expect, but I did know I would leave it for him to find me. I wasn't going to go out of my way to conjure him up. Dare I think, with Mardi Gras put to bed for a year, perhaps he would be too? I ambled around the city in fascination, with no particular place to go, just enjoying the people and places around me. It was a different world for me, and I wanted to soak up as much of it as I could. It would have been interesting to visit a decorative cemetery, but this was one of the places I knew better than to explore.

Finally, I rested on the circular bench surrounding the fountain at St. Louis Cathedral. I sat with my left foot firmly planted on the cement walk while my right leg was crossed over so I could hold on to it while sitting upright, watching people stroll by. Then he appeared. Once more, he sat on my right, mimicking my posture.

"Well, now, my Canadian client, I gather y'all have time now to give me my payment?"

He sounded downright pleased with this reversal of roles. Needless to say, I was somewhat apprehensive. His chilly presence was most unwelcome, even in the heat of the day. I shifted over a little on the marble bench, bending away from him.

"Here I am," I braved. "What's on your mind? Let's get this over with. I have a plane to catch." I hoped I sounded braver than I felt.

"The rumours of my sudden death are true. Did I tell you how I became a blobby mess on the side of an alleyway with no one there to care? No?" He leaned forward in great anticipation, readying himself to relate a blow-by-blow account of his death.

"No!" I interjected. "And I'm one of those that don't care! Let's move on with this."

He looked quite disappointed with my response and prepared to throw in his details anyway. He raised his head and nose and sniffled a little, making his bells jingle in sorrow.

"You're as feeling as the drunken dolt that ran over me, then backed over me just to see if he had indeed hit something. Verifying the fact he had, he roared off, leaving me lying there with my blood leaking out into my exposed guts and brain matter. I still had enough strength and brain left in me to write his licence plate number down in my blood."

Looking rather heroic from what little I could see beneath his mask, he continued, "They caught him. He still had little pieces of me on the bottom of his car."

Waiting and hoping I would gush forth with praise for his cleverness but receiving none, he gave a superior sniff and carried on. "My boyfriend was utterly devastated. We had no time for a final farewell kiss. He sat by my hospital bedside until the rising of my spirit and bewailed that fact. He felt so guilty that he was not with me that evening. I don't know where he was, but it was not his fault. He shouldn't have this guilt hanging around his neck for the rest of his earthly time. Using you, my friend, as my surrogate, I would like to give him one last sincere farewell kiss."

"Oh no!" I was quick with my reaction. "I don't swing that way. That'd be gross. I can't do that."

"No grosser than if you expected me to bussy up with a French kiss for darling Masie," he counter-offered with a smirk.

"Yes, but, I am not asking you to do that!"

"No, but you are the one that needs to give payment."

Under the bottom of the mask, I could see his mouth and mustache drawing up into a grin of utter satisfaction. He was in control of my payment and I didn't know his strength in the realm of conjure.

He jumped up, stood in front of me, and with his hands, he indicated I should jump up too.

"Up you get now, and over you go to Jackson Square. It's only a short distance. The arts and crafts show is underway, and as usual, my talented man has his watercolours for sale. He is a great artiste. His booth is number twenty. Front and centre, he is displaying a large painting of me in costume in this particular stance."

Jester then struck a pose, standing tiptoe on one foot, bent knee on the other, whilst holding a hoop on one arm and juggling four balls of Mardi Gras colours. "You can't miss it. Now, when you find him, you wait for me to enter you and place one resounding kiss on his lips. Once he receives it, he will know it is me coming at him and still loving him. It will be the kind of kiss that only the two of us experienced. You don't have to do anything but be there. I will handle the rest. Hear me?"

Oh, I heard him. How in Heaven's good grace could I pull this off?

I sauntered over to Jackson Square, taking the time to figure out a way to slide out of this agreement. No brilliant thoughts were forthcoming. I was aware of Jester only by the depression of the air around me, as I refused to look his way.

The park was busy with sellers and buyers, and all were happy. Music and laughter filled the area. I spied booth twenty almost immediately, and true to Jester's information, there, in bright colours on display, was a six-by-three-foot painting of him.

He whispered in my ear. Whispering that close wasn't necessary, he knew that. "There he is, my handsome blonde, sitting in his canvas chair, watching for prospective customers without me by his side."

Jester sent a longing smile in his direction. "Now, go up to him and introduce yourself. Tell him you have a message from his jester. Ask him to stand up. Wait for just a little until I have a chance to enter you. I'll take charge from there. You wait; just talk to him. I am new at this, so my entry may not be smooth. Got it?"

While he was steeling himself for an entry, I was steeling myself to run for an exit. I checked out the handsome blonde boyfriend and watched a performance unfold. The equally handsome dark owner of booth number twenty-one suddenly appeared from between the side flaps. He quietly approached Blonde from behind. He bent down and put his hands around his neck, then slid his arms down his chest.

Blonde responded with a delightful laugh. He threw his head back and, with one hand, pulled handsome Dark's head over him and a deep meaningful kiss ensued. Blonde stood up; a few words and hand caresses were exchanged, and they romantically disappeared behind the booths.

Jester broke the silence of act one. "The bastard!" Not blasphemy in the name of the Lord. "He's taken up with Trevor! So soon! How could he? He should still be mourning me! Come on!"

In a whirlwind of icy cold, he moved me along at a fair clip, and I found myself standing in front of booth number twenty. To my amazement, Jester moved over to a shelf displaying small paintings depicting an assortment of New Orleans scenes. He steadied himself flat-footed, no twinkle toes, raised an arm and swished it through the line of canvasses. Nothing happened. His arm carried right on through. He stood his ground, growled, and seemed to be concentrating. Once more, he brought his arm along the row. The world carried on. The crowd moved, and the music played.

Jester twirled about, appearing to concentrate on lowering his spiritual thermometer, studied the line of paintings, growled some more, and tried again. With one fell swoop, they all tumbled over like a line of dominoes.

The clatter and commotion brought not only the eyes and condemnation of the passing crowd upon me, but also the two handsome ones hurrying forth as they tucked in their shirts.

"What the fuck! What you doin', man?" yelled Blonde as he made for my direction, followed closely by his new best friend. They were not extending the Big Easy friendly welcome I had come to know and love.

I held my hands up, palms outward in defence mode, as I took three steps backwards. "I didn't do it! The shelf just gave way!" That was the only excuse I had in my arsenal.

"You tryin' to tell me they just went flyin' off the shelf all by themselves?"

"Well, in a manner of speaking, yes." That was my story, and I was sticking to it quite successfully until Jester decided he had other acts of revenge.

He approached the painting of himself, and I suppose after knocking over the shelf of canvasses, he felt strong. He calmed himself and proceeded to try the same tactic with the painting. It was to no avail. I suppose the painting was too heavy or his abilities were not as honed as he thought. While I was in the middle of negotiating with the recent twosome, Jester proclaimed he had changed his payment.

Now I had an out was my hopeful thought. He decided a kiss was unwanted. His plan now was to ruin the painting, and my help in accomplishing this goal was what he demanded. I sorely needed to let him know this was not up for negotiation. He had wanted the kiss, but now he didn't. He had cancelled our agreement, and I should be home free, but how could I speak with him while he was fussing around the large portrait and the twosome was circling me as if trying to decide what part of me to pummel while the crowd of onlookers was growing in size and temperament.

I felt a tingle in my right arm and found myself being dragged over to the painting that stood alone on its very own easel. Jester found the energy to control my arm in a spastic sort of way and attempted to knock it over. I resisted as he continued to call on his force. This resulted in a rather open-handed stroking of the canvass on my part.

The two and the crowd stood flabbergasted in wonder as I performed like a jerky marionette while talking nonsense to myself.

"Move your hand, man. Make a fist. Knock it over!"

"I can't." I was grasping for excuses. "I'm left-handed."

I felt a low-energy shockwave course through my upper body as my right arm went limp and my left arm gained strength. It shot out and punched a ragged tear through the centre of the painted Jester's torso. The canvas fell to the ground, and wasting little time, the electric jolt travelled down to my left foot, which kicked out, then stepped on canvas Jester.

Boyfriends and crowd stared in wide-eyed disbelief. Only I could see Jester clap the ethereal dust off his hands, as strings of beads jangled happily to and fro. His smirk of satisfaction was aimed not at me but at his former boyfriend as he arced his arms in the air, raised high on his tippy toes, and *snap*! He vaporized.

There I stood, in the middle of a crowd of shoppers and vendors looking for answers and justification for my misdemeanour. Handsome Blonde picked up the slack.

"You just bought one large painting and several small ones. Get your ass over here while I write up the damage costs."

I did, feeling fortunate he was a lover, not a fighter. I paid big time in US currency. That hurt more than the knuckles of my left hand.

As soon as possible, I junked the artiste mess I was forced to carry away from the arts and crafts show and slunk back to my hotel to retrieve my luggage.

My return flight to Lester B. Pearson Airport in Toronto was blessedly uneventful. Jester did not appear for a final, "now we are settled," which is customary and only polite. I didn't mind in the least. When all was said and done, I learned a valuable lesson: never, never to do a payment switch, no matter how tempting. But I would do New Orleans again at a non-Mardi Gras time.

4 MATCHMAKER

I ENJOY MY WORK at the Central Ontario Detective Agency. Assignments are varied and they seldom put me in danger. I never yearned to catch a killer or be a hero even in my younger, more dashing days. A *Columbo* or *a Law and Order* facsimile I was not. My assignments are more like the one I found waiting for me early one morning a while ago.

A prominent provincial figure had met her demise quite unexpectedly due to a heart attack. Those inclined had paid their respects, and she was about to make her journey to her final resting place. The procession would proceed north along Younge Street to Mount Pleasant Cemetery, flanked by federal black vehicles moving slowly through red lights, as was her due, with flashers flashing and motorcycle police on the left and right.

I was to meet with my assigned partner, Mellie, at the funeral establishment to receive instructions as to where we should be placed throughout the cemetery grounds. In this day and age, we must be on the lookout for unbalanced nasties or those of other political persuasions, if there's a difference.

I was running late. I had nicked my neck while shaving, so one spot of crimson demanded I change the white shirt and retie the tie. This seemed to be my way of moving from point A to B, but I did enter the building with time to spare, and I proceeded down the dignified carpeted hall, making a left turn into the viewing area. The first alert that something was amiss was when my brain cells registered the room was void of mourners. Soft organ music soothed the empty room containing twin caskets lovingly covered with a multitude of flower arrangements with perfumed smells and loving remembrances. Not exactly what one would choose for the last memories of our politician. This must be the wrong room. I should have turned right instead of left.

I quickly did a roundabout and retreated three or four steps when a grandmotherly voice stilled me. But the room was empty! *Oh no!* I thought. *Here I go again!*

"Please wait a moment, won't you, young man?"

Now if your grandmother asked that of you, you would wait just a moment, wouldn't you?

I turned with a snap of my shiny black shoes and looked back at the well-varnished caskets. Standing in between, with a hand on each, was a well-dressed grandmother. She was rather short in stature, with an ample bosom hiding under a peach-coloured dress belted at the waist. It hung unevenly at the hem due to the contour of the rumpled shape that nature bestows upon some women in their later years. Her snowy white hair was short and curled. Unfortunately, someone had applied too much rouge on her sallow cheeks, but all in all, the kindness on her face indicated she deserved all the accolades that lay upon the caskets. *Why two?* I wondered. Why did I wonder and ask?

"Two caskets and only you?"

"No, no, it is my husband of sixty years and me." She gazed lovingly at the top of one of them and patted it firmly. "A matching set," she proudly informed me.

"I don't have time, ma'am. I'm sorry. I'm already late for the politician's burial. Perhaps another time." How flippant and insincere was that? But she took me literally.

"Oh, another time will do just fine, then. I am a wandering ghost. I always did like to wander about, but poor Barney is a spirit, so he can't leave the hospital. If you could please make your way to Toronto General Hospital in the next week or so and take us on as your next otherworldly clientele, we will be very quick with our otherworldly payment, I assure you. Go to the third-floor chapel and we will find you. Barney will be so pleased. Don't take on another before us. You won't now, will you!"

She didn't ask, she stated. With fingers intertwined, she clasped them under her chin and gave me the smile that lights up a grandmother's face when she looks at a grandson. Yes, she had me hooked. I am a weakling when it comes to grandparents.

"I must go. I'm really late." I did a sidestep slide out of the room.

As the door silently swung closed behind me, I heard her voice softly trailing off. "We never voted for her. She was a crook, a liar, and a lesbian!"

Not a very grandmotherly statement in today's climate, but on the other hand, her generation held a detrimental point of view on such matters. Still, I found myself with the visual image of her lovingly stroking the coffin containing her husband's last earthly remains. Sixty years of marriage—not all of them blissful, I expect—said something about her time bound to Earth.

I caught up with Mellie as she was walking to the third car behind the hearse. She handed me the lookout position assignments for when we reached the cemetery. Mellie was a sweetheart at covering for my failure in time management. She looked somewhat better than she had in the past couple of weeks. Her skin was not as blotchy, eyes not as sunken. Mellie had hoped her partner would become her wife in the not too distant future, but unforeseen circumstances and a younger skinny twerp had interrupted those plans.

"Did you notice her?" she queried under her breath as we continued to our vehicle.

Was this a trick question? When in doubt, answer the question with a question.

"Did you?"

Mellie rolled her eyes, not buying my strategy for a millisecond.

"I noticed her at the public viewing in the provincial dais and again here not long ago. She was in the hall of the family viewing suite. She didn't go in, so she's not family. Not dressed for the occasion either: jeans, oversized grey hoodie with a pouch on the front, no markings or logo, white sneakers, large dark glasses, head low, strings of blonde hair hanging down . . . Trying to be inconspicuous but was conspicuous as hell."

Mellie's detection skills were second only to mine.

We had reached our designated car, and as the driver opened the door, I muttered, "I'll keep a lookout." I was feeling as conspicuous as hell.

I was perched far from the milling crowd surrounding the gravesite, which gave Mellie the duty of driving an inconspicuous car slowly around the twisting drive. I knew her arthritis would be saying hello to her hands in this weather, so one helps as one can by taking the worst assignment.

Two tall pines on the rise gave me good cover and an excellent view of the immediate area and the west entrance. A mist was settling into a fine rain, not enough to chase away the mourners, just enough to fog up vision. It was then I spotted a grey hoodie turning the curve as she jogged slowly along the gravel path. Thanks to Mellie, I was on alert. I delayed giving radio contact until I deemed if there was a sign of immediate danger. She veered off the path and trudged up the rise not far from my station. She turned when she was parallel to me but remained oblivious to my presence. She watched the funeral proceedings below in sadness. It was obvious the wetness she was wiping off her face with the back of her hand was not caused by the heavy dew in the air.

We waited. We watched. When the graveside service came to a close, she made her way down the hill to the path with care and jogged away slowly. She moved toward the west gate, reversing the path she had taken when she came in.

When I met up with official partner Mellie once more, I informed her of what I had observed. "Yes, I saw her: the mysterious grey hoodie. She watched the proceedings from the hillside and then left. We'll make a note."

A note was duly made, and no further action was deemed necessary.

Shortly thereafter, Mellie and I were assigned to another case involving the deceased politician. We often were called to work together as we found it effortless to role-play the drama of whatever the case called for. She was a foil, was Mellie. She could be my wife, mother, sister, or I could be yang to her yin.

I had suspicions that this new case might have the elements of a family affair, but we needed to detect it. The dearly departed politician, Sybil Morley, had left behind a trio of Morley siblings, who seemed to have a good understanding of her valuables and her public life, but little it seemed about her private life—or if they did, they were not about to enlighten us. Some things were missing, they reported, handing us a rather short list arranged in alphabetical order. One personal computer, two journals, three small paintings, four photo albums, five jewellery pieces... *and a partridge in a pear tree*? Just kidding!

No break-in had occurred. No mess or damage had been made. Of course, they knew we would want to dust for fingerprints. After explaining that fingerprinting procedures are done by police investigators and not us privates, and it was messy, they decided against it.

"Let's keep things private," they insisted.

And so, Mellie and I set forth with interviews and pounding the pavement by showing pawn shop owners photos of the goods and checking online selling sites for the missing items.

After more than a boring week of work, my curiosity about my encounter with the grandmotherly ghost at the funeral home got the better of me. She and her loving spirit husband, Barney, would be waiting, so off I went to the third floor chapel of old TGH.

I sat on a side pew to best keep an eye on the back door entrance, in case another earthly mortal entered to find solace. I would then be alert enough to keep my voice to a prayer-enhanced whisper or wait until they exited. We all have our exits and our entrances. It wasn't long until my two prospective clients wafted forth. They softly sat in forward-facing pews: she on one and he right behind her. They sat sideways, not forward in the pews, so they were both side by side facing me. How cleverly staged was that? They obviously had this meeting planned.

She put her right hand on the back of her pew, nodded her head at him, and, in an "I was right" way, stated, "See, I told you he would come!"

He turned to her and put his hand on top of hers. It went right through to the pew itself. Ghosts and spirits vaporize right through each other. I wondered if they received an electric buzz. Forgive me for my sacrilegious musings; we mortals have our moments.

"You explain our need to him, Barney dear. Your strength is greater than mine. It always has been." She gave him a look made of all sweet accord.

He nodded his agreement, turned to me, and commenced his tale. "Have you wondered how we came to our end together, young man?"

"Not really. We all come to our end eventually. If you reach that point at the same time as your life partner, that means neither one of you is left with heartbreak. Sounds good to me."

My nonchalant sarcasm sailed along right over his head. He carried on.

"COVID-19, of course. Very painful and unpleasant it was at the time, but by the grace of God, only a short spell. We were in separate rooms but didn't care, as we were not aware of anything anyway. We had heard how terrible it was for victims of COVID-19 dying alone. It doesn't matter: you don't know or care who is there anyway. I wish families and loved ones knew that. It would save them a lot of anguish and guilt. We had no one to be there that we cared for, except our daughter. We outlived most of our friends and family. We rose together, and that was a wonderful thing. No one knew but us."

He looked over at his wife, and they exchanged a communication that only two soulmates could read. How fortunate they were.

He gave a carry-on sigh. "It's about our daughter, you see. She's all alone. She would tell us she was fine, but toward the end, we could sense there was a change in her life and she was not living a satisfactory existence. She has a good profession. She is a lawyer with an up-and-coming tech company."

I believe he noticed my eyes glazing over in disinterest about the same time he noticed his soulmate jiggling about on her pew.

"Getting right to the point," he hurried on. "She needs to find love in her life, someone who can love her for herself and she can love back. Someone who will share her interests and who can give her a new lease on life. She has lost us, and it appears she has no other outlet except for helping at the kennel club."

Right away my wary detective radar detected a matchmaker in progress. It needed to be nipped in the bud.

"Hold it right there, sir. I have been divorced four times but already have found another willing lady to be number five. I'm no candidate for your daughter." Does the Lord forgive liars?

He pulled his shoulders and his chin back in shock. "In no way did I mean to infer such a union, lad. You would be too unstable and malleable for her. She needs a strong and forceful hand. Try to locate a gentleman on the cusp of retirement with a good pension and has an interest in . . ." He looked over at his wife. "Help me out here, Joannie."

"Dogs, computers, and cooking, because she can't cook. The best thing she ever made for dinner was reservations," she quipped quickly.

"You can give me the details, but first let me tell you what I would like for payment. How did you find out about me and the weakness in my aura? Can you check around there, wherever you are, and find out why this happened to me? This has always been a burning question for me."

Barney became quite agitated at my request. He looked at Joannie, and it was obvious to both of us that not only was Joannie fading away into the great beyond, but a group of seekers in need of prayer were entering the chapel.

"I sought you out after hearing from satisfied customers, who were able to move on because of your help. I have no idea how you came to be so blessed or how I could find out why. Meet our daughter and help her out. You will receive the love of your life.

"Marilyn Bowman, 202 Circle Avenue Etobicoke. Lawyer at Teckno Cancon," he hurriedly relayed as they both misted away.

I had a great urge to grab out at him, shout out at him, and tell him null and void! I did not want another love in my life, but they were gone. The recent arrival of a tearful family in mourning had now moved up near the front to the chapel cross. They did not need to witness a lone man acting like he was off his rails, shouting at nothingness.

I left TGH feeling rather disgruntled. So often I leave myself open to the unknown. I bring it on myself, and I am fully aware I am a sucker for the geriatric clientele. Some people play with golfing buddies; I play with ghosts.

~

Barney and Joannie did not top my priority list as Mellie and I continued our detection into the affairs of the missing items of our dearly departed politician. It appeared she was not as missed as her items. The government, being as it is, swiftly replaced her seat on the same side of the aisle, and all things political wrangled on as usual.

Mellie likes to wander through Internet sites for reasons of her own, and I prefer to wander out in the field—in this case, through pawnshops and outside markets—for reasons of my own. We keep our reasons to ourselves and maintain a great relationship. When working as a team, we often arrange to meet and exchange our information over a coffee or something a little more invigorating, depending on the yardarm.

Was it happenstance or a ghostly shove that I found myself, one sunny afternoon, coasting along Rexdale Boulevard when my GPS lit up an entrance to Circle Avenue? That jogged my memory to the request by dear Barney and Joannie. On impulse and with no tailgater behind, I pulled a quick right to Circle Avenue and slowly meandered down a quiet suburbia maze. You know how these streets go: little winds and turns that shoot off to other streets, appearing and disappearing just enough to do their duty in keeping you slow and mindful that children live and play there.

Number 202 soon came into sight on my left. It was a cookie-cutter house, one of a series of six that took up the whole housing development, dating, I reckoned by the designs, to the 1980s. The house was well maintained, with mature trees and established gardens along the edge of the house front and driveway. I halted automatically, then forced myself to continue at a crawl. Was I seeing what I thought I was seeing? But I was only looking at a butt. She was on her hands and knees, weeding and digging vigorously. She turned slightly and gave me a side view: blue jeans, a grey hoodie, front pouch, and blonde hair tied back, but some straggling forward across her thin face.

I stepped on the accelerator to hurry around the upcoming curve and out of sight before stopping to consider the scene. I adjusted my side and rear-view mirror to sneak a peek at her. As she dug away, I could just make out the top of her back as she continued along the row of flowers on all fours. An energetic couple fast-walking by me with their Doberman gave me a look that hinted they were taking note of not only me but my licence plate as well. My time was limited.

Grey Hoodie suddenly made a recognizable manoeuvre: she bent one knee and, using a hand on the knee, raised herself and held her back. I felt her pain. It arrives with that age group. Could Barney and Joannie's lonely unloved daughter be our grey-hoodie phantom? I had to consider the connection and how to lay this information on Mellie in a sensical way, although Mellie was quite used to my nonsensical explanations.

Grey Hoodie was at the funeral parlour, so were Barney and Joannie, her dearly departed from COVID-19, and Ms. Politician, from heart failure.

Grey Hoodie was at Mount Pleasant, so was Ms. Politician. Were Barney and Joannie there as well? Do I detect on my own and risk the wrath of Mellie or tell her my hound dog theory and have her growl at me? Mellie would not approve one way or the other. She worked from the facts-only approach, while I dithered in the what-ifs and perhaps.

I had to tighten the leash on my thoughts, as I was not sure where it was going. I left Circle Avenue, giving the returning dog walkers a nod just to establish a confident "I belong here too" look.

I did a little online detecting and established the fact that the COVID=19 couple were not comfortably embedded at Mount Pleasant but were, facts only, in a family plot near

Alliston. The family farm in the area now sported a well-designed subdivision much like the one Grey Hoodie now lived in. My plot was not thickening. Time to call Mellie.

Mellie's cell rang up to the allotted fourth ring before she whispered annoyingly, "This better be good, Dan. I'm off the clock!"

Good old Mellie . . . always so diplomatic. "Sorry, I didn't know. Where are you?"

"At the health clinic, in the middle of my pain-management course for arthritis. Have you got something?"

I did now. A light bulb just shimmered in the dark recesses of my mind. "Of course, partner, would I bother you if I didn't?" I fudged.

Later that afternoon, we secured an inside booth at our favourite Tim Hortons, and I laid out my plan. "This is the way of it." How official was that! "I found Grey Hoodie."

Mellie was about impressed as she usually gets. She bobbed her head in affirmation, meaning "carry on." The connection between Grey Hoodie and Politician Morley's stolen property was very thin, and I wasn't sure Mellie would buy into it, but I valiantly carried on.

Informing her I had located her name, place, and address because of good detecting, I laid out my plan. Mellie would come to a screeching halt if she ever caught a whiff of my ghostly encounters.

"You, Mellie, have to take the lead in this. You get to know Grey Hoodie, aka Marilyn Bowman, or is it the other way around? There may be a connection between her and the politician's stolen items. If you could get inside her house, you could check things out."

We scoped out Bowman's abode as discreetly as our detecting skills allowed, and it was not long before we found her once more tending her flower bed.

With pamphlets from the health clinic on classes for arthritis pain management, Mellie got out of the car and approached her. I was not privy to the conversation that ensued, but Mellie must have been doing a hell of a job, as within five minutes, she had an invite inside. Where we went from there was up to Mellie.

I waited. The fast-walking couple with Doberman walked by and back again. Quizzical looks were not kind, and neither was my bladder. Mellie was going a little overboard here. I was beginning to think dark thoughts when she mercifully appeared with a spring in her step and a smile on her face, the first I had seen in a long time. I could not bark at her for taking so long when she looked so successful.

"Drive on," she ordered. "I'll fill you in." She turned and waved goodbye to our suspect. What was that all about?

"We're not going any farther than the first Tims or McDs," I told her. "A pit stop, then a tell over a coffee."

"Fine," she agreed. "By the way, I've never asked you: Do you like dogs?"

Now, where was she going with this? From arthritis lectures to dogs? I hesitated, thinking my way around an answer without a commitment.

"As long as they're not Dobermans." That was the best I could do on short notice, and a swerve at the next light brought us into a Tims.

Over Tims darkest brew, Mellie related her detective results. While she seemed quite moved by it all, I was quite concerned. At the time, she knew never to get caught in the emotion of the cases, and naturally, I'm one to give that kind of straightforward advice, aren't I? We seemed to have been caught in a role-reversal.

Facts at our fingertips now were not much more than Marilyn Bowman was going to join Mellie at the arthritis lectures if Mellie would join her for a visit to the Canadian Kennel Club.

"Come on now," she chided me. "Don't we all love dogs as long as they aren't Dobermans, and why is that by the way?"

"And no, by the way, if I loved dogs, I would have one. And as you very well know, I don't!"

She just smiled and waited.

"Who are you and what did you do with Mellie?" This person before me was not being factual. She was teasing me. Why?

Finally, she gave a shrug and a "well, okay then" sigh, and I became her father confessor.

"You see"—she twisted her napkin—"it only took a couple of minutes for us to know we were both lez. Then she invited me into her house and gave me a confession that she had been the politician Sybil Morley's partner. In the closet, they were. Before I knew it, I was giving her my sordid story of being dumped by my partner of five years for a young tramp."

"Just the facts, ma'am," I prompted her. "Of the case, that is. I don't need a play-by-play of your love life. I need you to get back on the scent of tracking down the politician's missing items. Bowman has them, correct?"

"I couldn't ask. Really now! The plan was for me to get to know her, take her to the clinic, maybe become friends, and we could search the house. You wanted me to do all that while you were out there, snoozing in the car?"

Oh, how apt she was at turning the table. Mellie was back.

It finally dawned on me that something was afoot—or, perhaps I should say, "apaw"—when the case of the politician's purloined pieces had become an investigation solely under the auspices of Mellie. Whenever I inquired about a meeting of the minds, she was either running to or running from the CKC (Canadian Kennel Club) or the BHCC (Basset Hound Club of Canada) with Ms. Marilyn Bowman, our number one suspect.

I knew it was time to confront her and hear if she was mixing business with pleasure, and I didn't mean for the love of the dogs.

"Now see here, Mellie!" I rehearsed in front of my mirror. I intended to be stern with her, even though she was old enough to be my big sister. I sent her a text with a time to meet once again at our favourite Tims. I ordered her a walnut crunch doughnut, knowing that was her favourite, and a coffee before she arrived. A little butter never hurts. I watched her as she strode across the parking lot, enter the side door, and plunk down across from me.

Before I could utter my rehearsed line, she spoke.

"Okay, it's arranged."

I waited. She bit into the walnut crunch. She chewed and sipped her coffee.

"This is the way it will go down. Marilyn has to go up to Alliston to pick up a basset hound and her new litter of pups."

Visions of nastiness danced in my head. And I should care about this because? Will she visit Barney and Joannie? I was not very fond of Mellie at the moment. She had left me out of our case and had forsaken me for a litter of puppies and a suspect. All I had was a ghost and a spirit that were looking to be disappointed.

"Are you paying attention?" She shot me a dagger look over chipmunk cheeks full of the last of the crunch.

"Uh-huh." I placed my elbow on the table and rested my chin on my hand, then stared straight at her and waited.

"We need an SUV to transport the dogs down to Marilyn's house." I noted the "we." "We will meet at Marilyn's; I will introduce you as a friend. You will drive her up to get the hounds in your SUV. She will give me her house key, and I will be out at PetSmart, purchasing the essentials for the canine family's stay. The whole trip will take several hours, so I will have plenty of time to dig around and see if Mar has the property."

I was alerted to the name change. We had leap-frogged from Grey Hoodie to Bowman to Marilyn to Mar, and then to property sans stolen, quite quickly. I left it alone for now.

"You could have run this by me first, Mellie." I knew I sounded peevishly pouty, but in fact, that was how I felt.

"I'm telling you now!"

I waited. Waiting can wear some people down; they tend to want to fill the void.

Mellie wrapped her hand around her coffee cup, hiding the Tims logo, drew patterns on the table with her wet spoon, and gave a sigh.

"We've really hit it off, Dan. I think we've become a match. It frightens both of us so soon after we've both been hurting. Not only that, she's in the dark as to what we are doing."

Ah, that we included me. Now I felt better. Mellie had a dilemma; she alone would have to fix it, but the crumbles around the edges looked like they would fall on my dilemma. If she was to be Marilyn's true love, bully for them. However, I was sure that was not the lasting life adventure Joannie meant me to find for her all-alone daughter. A spirit and a ghost together may be capable of conjuring up a payment on demand that would affect my love life until my forever after, considering my four times plus lie. Would I be doomed to be followed by a gay stalker?

"Very well," I acquiesced. "I'll go and get the bitch."

Mellie assured me they would not leave a mess of any type or description behind in my SUV. I got that in writing, for what it was worth.

And so it was that I ventured forth to the countryside just north of the pretty town of Alliston with Mar. She was friendly enough, with small talk about her dearly departed parents and the family plot near Alliston, where three generations of Bowmans now resided. She chatted about her love for horses and dogs going back to her younger years when she grew up on the farm. I was thankful it was dogs we were picking up and not horses.

The family who lived in the countryside home were over the moon about Ms. Basset's accomplished litter and relieved that Mar had agreed to take them off their hands until weaned. There was quite a fuss made about the whole affair. From my uneducated point of view, staring down at the enclosed smelly area, I saw only a squirming mess of white, tan, and black movement. Floppy ears, sorrowful eyes, and oversized paws reigned. It was beyond my comprehension how anyone could devote time and energy to such a muddle. Why couldn't this loving countryside family keep this Basset family? Well, it appeared their beagle was due for her litter any day now. I do believe they all needed some sort of birth control.

I stood aside while Mar and country family bedded Mother Basset and litter in the back of my pristine SUV. I was assured the sides of the wire enclosure were high enough to keep all within the confines of the bed. That was true until one or two climbed on top of their mother and toppled over and out. It took four stops and Mar holding two of the escapees to complete the exceedingly long journey back to 202 Circle Avenue.

Mellie met us as we pulled into the driveway. As I flipped the hatch, she gave me a heads-up nod that indicated our trip was not in vain. She made all sorts of unMellie-like noises as she proceeded to help Mar unload the Basset family.

"Here, hold this one. He's escaping." She thrust one of the little squirms into my chest and left me standing there. It was all I could do to hold him as he wiggled and turned upside down and every which way but loose. The two Ms ignored my fate, and in smooth practiced style, they delivered all else into the house. There I stood, with this little thing still squirming about as I focused in horror at the mess in my brand-new SUV. It was covered in hound drool and slime, among other substances I was afraid to identify. Detail time on Mellie's credit card.

I hung on to him as best as I could and made for the house. This was a new venture for me, so I had to detect the interior surroundings for further information. First and foremost, I needed to liaison with Mellie to ascertain our next plan of attack. Opening the door showed me a scene that was akin to the Keystone Cops in miniature: little paws were scooting about, jumping here and there; Mother Basset was howling; her children were yipping; and the two adults in charge were bowled over in laughter, trying to catch them.

Time to wait once more. I sat down on the nearest living room hostess chair. I found myself fondling this pup's oversized floppy ears that hung down on each side of his face. I was not about to let go of him and allow him to take part in the ongoing confusion. His eyes looked up. They were so sad. His mouth turned down. He rubbed his very wet nose against my shirt and gave a tiny squeak. He was kinda cute, and I was kinda taken with him until I felt a growing warm wetness on the front of my jeans. It registered what else this pup was doing.

I stood up and held him at arm's length. "He peed on me!" And he was still streaming.

Mellie was on her back on Mar's sofa, knees up, holding her stomach. Her eyes were wet. Her laughs were so backed up, they had trouble escaping. Mar was on the floor leaning against the sofa in the same condition.

Mar managed to wheeze out, "Should name him Puddles."

"No," Mellie countered. "Sooner! 'Cause he'd sooner do it there than here!" Laughter abounded, but not by me.

Perhaps it was time for me to call the men in white coats to come and take them away. I was not amused.

I placed the tiny pup down beside his mom and took my exit, front door slamming!

It took a couple of days for Mellie to get her act together and call for a Tims meeting. She appeared to be her old self and settled in with just the facts. She opened her notepad and began scrolling.

"I found exactly what the politician's siblings were looking for. They were hiding in plain sight." She read them off as she counted them on her fingers. "One personal computer, two journals, three small paintings, four photo albums, and five jewellery pieces."

Mellie looked across the square Formica table at me with pain in her eyes. "Dan, you have to take over on this one. Mar and I have developed a relationship that we both want to hang on to. How can I tell her what I have been doing all this time? She has every right to hate me, and she will."

"Could be." I had no intention of laying on butter. "If she does, then it wasn't as serious as you thought." And Barney and Joannie won't hate me. "I found her, Mel; I asked you to do the arthritis thing. You got tangled from there. I can explain being assigned to the Morley case; you jump in whenever you want, or not. Let her explain how she came across these items, and we can take it from there depending on her reaction. How does that sound?"

Mellie bent her head, clasped her hands, and rubbed her thumbs together. She hesitated just slightly, then made her decision. "You're right! There can't be any secrets if I want to make a life with her. She has to know what I do for a living, even if it's not for much longer."

That was news to me. I looked at her and waited for more information.

"Don't give me that look. You know I intend to seek a life of luxury in another year or so." She smiled a little at her joke. "All right then. I'll text Mar and see if we can drop over tomorrow for lunch. We'll bring subs. Mar doesn't cook."

"Sounds good." I rose from our corner table and turned for the door. Then in my best Columbo imitation, I scratched my forehead with the back of my thumb and turned around. "One more thing, ma'am. Does Mar still have those puppies?"

———

We arrived at 202 Circle Avenue with subs tied up with a twirl. Mar showed happy-face signs at seeing Mel and gave me a nod of recognition. I had been coached not to wait too long. We were waved into the kitchen, and I put the subs on the table. Mar was ripping open the packaging as Mel dove into a cupboard and produced three plates. She gave me go-ahead stares as she opened the fridge door and stuck her head in, searching for liquid refreshments. That was her inventive way of avoiding eye contact with Mar.

I spoke. "Where's Momma Basset and her six little ones, Mar?"

The ripping stopped, and I was given an inquisitive look. "In the spare room. The door's closed. You seemed so upset by them when we brought them, I put them out of the way."

I tried for nonchalance. "Just wondering how much that little peeing one has grown. Could I see him?"

"How will you know which one he is?"

"He has two tan spots on his nose, like large freckles." I twirled a finger in front of my nose for emphasis.

Mar disappeared. I heard a door down the hall open and then the faint sound of squeaky puppy noises. Meanwhile, Mel turned and looking up, gave me a dirty face look and mimed, "What do you think you're doing?" Mar returned with the two-freckled pup, slightly larger than last week but just as wiggly. I swear when he saw me, he remembered how he had christened me. Mar handed him over.

"Hey, little guy, how ya doing?" I snuggled him up on my shoulder. He licked my ear and sniffed my neck. His ears were flat, floppy, and still so velvety. His tail was swinging with a boogie beat. His tiny back legs and ungainly paws were scratching a quick Texas two-step on my chest.

"Time out!" Mar swooped him off me not so gently and whisked him away. "Wash your hands, softie. Lunchtime." I could hear him woofing for me.

As we sat in the brightly lit kitchen, munching on subs, I broached the tale of my clients, the siblings. "Once upon a time," I began, "there was a grey hoodie."

Mar waited. She heard me out in silence. Only her eyes shifted from me to Mel's downcast eyes when it seemed my message crunched a nerve.

When my soliloquy was as done as our subs, Mar looked at Mel, drew in a deep breath, and launched into her answer.

"I knew you had been looking through my personal belongings, Mel. Things were just a little off-kilter, you know? Moved a tiny bit too close to the edge of the shelf . . . a picture just a little not crooked. I thought it best to wait until we could have a mutual confession about where our feelings and trust would take us.

"Sybil and I were partners for ten years. Silent partners. Her two brothers and sister refused to acknowledge me. They convinced her if she made her lifestyle public, her political career would be kaput. Oh, people say they're open-minded, but not when it comes time to vote. I always had a key to her condo, and she had a key to this house. We would come and go as discreetly as we could. That's why I wore my grey hoodie and stayed back in the shadows at her funeral. I had a legitimate reason for being at the funeral home. My parents were there at the same time, but due to COVID-19, I was only allowed one short visitation."

Mar paused briefly and then continued when neither Mellie nor I did not attempt to interrupt.

"The items in question. Yes, I went to Sybil's condo, used my key to enter, and took them. The computer was the personal one she used for our communication. The journals were about our travels together. We would leave the country separately and meet up. She was a fanatic about daily writing. The paintings were done by local artists in the countries we visited. I bought them for her. No monetary value. The albums—if you care to see them if you haven't already—are pictures of where we travelled. The jewellery was mine. If she admired anything I was wearing, I would take it off and give it to her at the end of the evening. She did the same for me."

Mel reached out for her hand, and the squeeze was retaliatory. I left, sans Mellie.

I made solitary contact with the siblings to inform them that the stolen had been located. They were all for retrieval and going forth with charges of theft. I encouraged them to do so and ensured them I would gladly be a character witness in going public with all the forms of media we have, letting the country, indeed the world, know that our renowned politician was a trusted lesbian who had been betrayed and stolen from by her lesbian lover of ten years.

Thinking on this matter, the siblings backtracked and chose to let sleeping dogs lie. I mused over thoughts of sleeping basset hound puppies.

I left it to Mellie to give Mar the news. I thought it best to let the two of them tidy up their commitment without a third-party present. I took the opportunity to return once more to TGH and face the reaction of Barney and Joannie. I was aware that this was not the type of love for life Joannie had in mind for her only, lonely daughter Marilyn. She probably was never aware of Marilyn's political connection.

I was wary of their payment for my services. One is never sure how services will be rendered and the payment promised will be achieved. I sat in the designated pew in the third-floor chapel and waited. It was not a long wait. Barney and Joannie made their appearance in the same manner as before, each occupying their separate pew facing me. Barney shrugged his shoulders with hands raised, palms flat. Joannie refused to look at me.

"I explained to her," he started. "I told her it was Marilyn's life and attitudes in the world are different now. If she is happy, then all is right in her world. Why should we carry the burden of parenthood up and beyond our mortal time on Earth?"

He turned to his soulmate's ghostly apparition and became a little stern with her. Rather her than me.

"Come now, Joannie, Marilyn is not alone. This young gentleman did the best he could under the circumstances. He needs to go and get the love of his life now."

On that note, Joannie turned to face me. In resignation, she asked, "What has made you the happiest in the past few weeks, sir? Where have you been and what have you done that has given you comfort that you would like to have continued forward?"

That gave me thought. I scratched my ear in the thinking and imagined the slurp of a puppy's wet tongue and the feel of a floppy velvet ear against my cheek. I slowly smiled at Joannie. "That little basset hound pup, Mrs. Bowman? You think he could fill the void in my life?"

She flipped one hand in the air and put it back on her lap. "What would I know about such things? As Barney said, things in the world are different now. Dogs don't just run around the barnyard like they used to. They become family members with all the privileges of a person and none of the responsibilities."

It dawned on me: I did love that funny little wriggly ball of white, tan, and black, with the big sorrowful eyes, aforesaid drool, and extraordinary ears.

"Of course, of course. I do love him. Thank you for bringing that to my attention. Payment is sufficient."

I left as the two of them faded away never to be seen again. It took longer than usual to get back to 202 Circle Avenue, as Rexdale Boulevard was busy with end-of-the-day traffic. Finally, I pulled into the driveway to the vision of two butts on their knees working on the flower bed. It seemed all was calm at 202. They stood, trying to hide arthritic pain, and welcomed me forward. I wasted no time.

"It's about Ms. Basset's litter, Mar. When that little one with the two big freckles is weaned, I would like to take it off her—what is the correct word? Body? How do I go about doing that? Can I see him again right now?"

The two Ms exchanged looks, and Mel gave Mar a "see, I told you" nod.

"They're not here anymore. We took them back up to the boarding farm. They're pretty much weaned now, and the BHCC will issue their pedigree papers. They'll be picked up by the families who are buying them. All of them will make great show dogs." Marilyn delivered this oratory to me in official rhetoric with no eye contact.

"When did you take them back?" "Yesterday," Mellie volunteered. "I thought of calling you, but the day got away from me, sorry."

Lessons learned from my ghostly friends: I didn't wish to waste time and energy on the exasperation of bygone deeds.

Taking a clue from Batman on the case of rescuing his sidekick Robin, I hastened to my Batmobile and drove with abandonment north to the countryside of Alliston, desperate to be in time to stop the sale of my puppy love to some joker who would want him for show purposes.

To tie up my story, I will enlighten the mystery and inform you that I was in time to rescue my two-tan-freckled hound. A few months ago, I would have been horrified to learn the value of dogs; they were nothing but hound dogs. After his initial outrageous cost, there would be medical expenses and daily upkeep expenses, but then, there is my little basset hound with the sorrowful eyes and drooly jowls.

I took him by to show Mar and Mel and let them know I had rescued him from a life of show-and-tell.

"What did you name him?" Mar asked. "Puddles or Sooner?"

"Neither, Marilyn. I've christened him Barney."

Marilyn gave me a quizzical look. "My father," she said, "was Bernard, but everyone called him Barney."

"Is that so?" said I.

5 THE STASH

ONE OF THE ADVANTAGES of living close to the Scarborough Bluffs, on the east side of Toronto, is that Barney and I can take an enjoyable walk and not repeat the route for more than a month if we don't want to. We have, on occasion, stopped at the off-leash dog run, but Barney has let me know he prefers not to mingle with the rabble that hangs out there. With his short legs and tummy near the ground, he often is the victim of the long-legged ones jumping over and around him. With his enhanced ability to smell and his floppy ears designed to bring the smells closer, he is somewhat put off by the odour of the impure breeds. He is rather a prude about his royal basset hound lineage. We usually stay on leash and take ourselves down whatever path suits his fancy.

Not long ago, we took our stroll along the bluffs through the Rosetta McClain Gardens. It is one of the areas where you can not only enjoy the gardens, but you may look down on Lake Ontario from a glorious height. The view differs daily depending on the weather and where you happen to wander. On this particular day, the wind was mild; the rippling waves caused the surface to display a zigzag pattern on a whim. A few cumulus clouds appeared to be pasted in the sky at just the perfect spots. Barney had a full leash, and as usual, he pulled me along wherever he wished. His fastest waddle would never stir up a dust storm. He stopped suddenly and looked straight ahead as if he had spied an item to his liking. I looked his way and discovered it was to my liking as well.

I could only see her back from the waist up, as she was sitting on a short brick wall surrounded by a circular hedge and a rose bush display. Her head was bent forward. Her long brown hair flowed down her pale-yellow sleeveless blouse. It was tied back out of the way by a trailing red ribbon. She appeared to be quite young, I thought, looking down from my age group.

I followed Barney around the circular walk, and we stopped to observe her sketching attentively on an eight-by-eleven-inch art pad. At her sandaled feet was a large carryall.

I remained quiet, but Barney did not. He gave a sneeze and wagged his head to and fro, managing to throw his ears about and arc some drool. She looked up, not surprised but a little annoyed. I received the vibes that too many observers interrupt her work to ask intelligent questions like, *what are you doing? Are you drawing? Can I see?*

I didn't wait. I spoke. "Sorry to stare. You look quite lovely sitting there. Someone should be drawing a picture of you." As soon as I tripped over my tongue on that one, I realized it sounded like a pickup line.

She settled her drawing pad on her knees, which were well covered by a long floral skirt. She could have come from either of the last two centuries. Bending down, she rummaged through her oversized floral bag with one hand. It emerged holding a real camera, zoom lens and all.

"Here then." She held it out to me. "Take a couple of photos of me, and maybe someone will draw it later. Just push the button on the top right side."

This request took me by surprise, but Barney was sitting in his best obedient mode, so I moved forward and took the camera. After turning it upside, downside, and all around, I finally was able to sort out how to take a picture. Not an easy feat for someone who only takes random shots with a cell phone of sneaky people at a distance.

When I handed the camera back, she checked what I had captured and seemed satisfied. I attempted to make small talk, but that was to no avail. Her responses relied on yeses and nos. She took a few pictures from her perch. Long-range shots of flower beds, close-up shots of roses, and an interesting zoom of a bumblebee entering the centre of a tiger lily. It appeared Barney was getting his share of close-ups as well.

I bid her farewell, and she nodded. Barney and I carried on along the cobbled path heading toward the gazebo. As we passed the last circle of contained floral groupings and approached the area of wild plantings, I became aware of his presence.

I waited. Barney ignored him. That was a good sign. He spoke.

"She is my daughter."

Sometimes, it is best to just wait some more.

"I was a procrastinator, and now she is suffering for it."

It's my curiosity that's my downfall. I questioned, "I take it then that you are a ghost, not a spirit? And you are middle-aged, as she is too young to be the daughter of an old man. Well, usually," I added to avoid insulting him. "How did you meet your demise?" I ask that question early on in meetings as I like to steer clear of violent endings.

"Can we sit?" he asked. "I could use your detection skills to help her and her mother."

We had approached the gazebo, and as there appeared to be no other earthly souls about, it was a good place for him to tell his tale.

I sat first and appreciated his choice of sitting far enough away that his coldness did not interfere with my space.

"Aneurysm," he uttered once he felt comfortable enough to begin his telling. He was leaning forward, feet planted firmly on the planked floor, forearms on his thighs, and hands laced together between them. "Brain aneurysm. It came on suddenly. No warning. My wife, Ella, found me on the kitchen floor when it was too late to do anything about it."

Now. I am not an impatient man, nor am I one without empathy, however, I have been down this ghostly "tell me a story" path before and understand that the ghostly battery supply has its limits.

"Get to your need and payment part, sir. While I do have empathy with your situation, we both know your time is limited and you mustn't waste it."

He turned to me with a jerk of his head that showed an inner debate about whether he should be insulted or not. Deciding not, and noticing Barney already catching forty dog winks under the bench between my feet, he got to the help and payment part with just a few roundabout curves.

"My father had a house in Nottawa."

"Your father? He must be a good age. Does he still live there? Where is Nottawa?"

He stood up and glided, as only ghosts can do, toward me. Standing in front of me and looking down at Barney, he went into chastise mode. "How can I get to the help and payment part if you keep interrupting with irrelevant questions?"

"Sorry," said I, the sheep, as he gave me a look I recognized on his daughter's face when she was questioned about her drawing.

He continued, "My father was a miser. Well, stingy is a better description, I suppose. He took good care of my mother and me, but he had this obsession with squirrelling away money. He wouldn't use banks. 'They charge you,' he would say. Our small house was paid for. He paid upfront for everything that was needed, and he gloated when counting his leftover cash."

He stopped for a moment, put his hand on his chin, and gave me an analogy. "Do you remember Donald Duck had an uncle Scrooge McDuck? He would play with his money. He would throw it in the air and run the coins through his fingers. My father was something like that. He hid his money in the house in different spots, moving it about every so often. He kept track of every penny when we used pennies. When he gathered enough change to make one hundred dollars, he would cash it in for one bill. Mother and I never knew where he hid his stash. Mind you, as a kid, I looked in every nook and cranny. It became a game. Sometimes, I would find it, but when I looked again, it would have been moved to another unknown location. I never found the last one."

He glided back over to his initial side of the gazebo and sat down on his former spot. I refrained from commenting.

"He died at a ripe old age five years ago. Be it the pack a day he smoked to the end or not, no one cared. Surprisingly, he had a will. He left the house and contents to Mother. There was no mention of a mother lode of cash hiding anywhere on the property. That was all well and good, except that at the time, Mother was showing signs of Alzheimer's. My daughter, Viv, and I had concerns about her living alone in the house in Nottawa, so against her wishes—and mind you, she could be a strong-minded woman regardless of what side of the track her mind was on—we managed to get her to move down here with us. You see, I was working in Toronto, and Viv was hoping to enter classes in the Arts Department at Toronto University."

He sat up in boastful pride and continued. I was bursting to find out where Nottawa was but held my tongue.

"Viv is in her second year in fine arts and literature. Now here's the problem my procrastination caused: I had not looked after our monetary affairs very well. Contrary to popular belief, our government system does not cover all medical needs. A caregiver came in to be with Mother when we were not at home. I was in the middle of arranging a psychiatric assessment for her. If the court could deem her unfit and turn the estate over to me, we could manage things. I could sell or rent the house to pay our bills. Viv has university tuition costs and living expenses that still need attending to.

"That took longer than anticipated, as during the first two visits with the psychiatrist, Mother appeared quite within the bounds of normalcy. After the third visit and the psychiatrist conferring with her family doctor back home, affairs were finally turned over to me, signed, sealed, and delivered. I had time for one relieved sigh before my demise happened. I had no will. I had left Viv and my wife in the lurch. They now have to begin the legal process all over again.

"It was not likely anyone would want to rent in Nottawa, but we could, in all likelihood, sell due to the growth just north of us."

Where in the hell is Nottawa? thought I, *Get on with it, man!*

He looked up at the trellis top of the circular gazebo with eyes as sad as Barney's. "If I only had a will! Nothing can be moved or sold out of the house until legal ownership is established."

My turn to talk, I decided. "I'm still not aware of what you want from me, nor do I know where Nottawa is. You'd better hurry. Twilight time is approaching."

"Yes, yes, you are correct, of course. Nothing in my father's will mentioned his stash of cash. The money is in the house somewhere. I had racked my brains looking and trying to think like him." He stopped and looked at me with questions in his eyes. "Can that cause an aneurysm?"

"A doctor, I am not! Carry on, carry on!" I urged.

"Viv has a key to the house. If you play your cards right, she will give it to you. Go up to the house and search using all your excellent detective skills. The house is old. It was built sometime in the 1940s. Nothing has changed since the 1970s. It's a mess, with many little hidey holes he could have used for his personal banking system. Find that stash somehow! Viv and her mother need the money. It is there somewhere. When they get the house legally, they can sell it and someone else will eventually find it."

He suddenly stopped and, to my way of thinking, changed the topic. At the time, I thought it had little meaning. "Have you ever heard of Stringbean Akeman?"

I gave a negative head shake.

"He sang and performed at the Grand Ole Opry way back when, with Grandpa Jones and the Gang. He didn't believe in banks either. He hid his money in the little shack he and his wife, Estelle, lived in. Word got around about that. On November 19, 1973, they were both shot by two young men looking for his stash. It wasn't found until 1996, when a new owner was doing renovations and found it hidden behind a brick in the chimney. By that time most of it had deteriorated and was useless. I am fearful someone will go in and wreak havoc looking for it, or in years to come, someone will find it all ruined. Just saying."

"And payment? And Nottawa?" I was just saying, again.

He looked annoyed and paler than Casper the Friendly Ghost. "Viv will give you the payment. Nottawa is south of

Collingwood. Take Highway 26 to Sideroad 34." He waved me off. "You have a GPS; use it."

"Before you leave," I quickly said, "I have a question for you."

He looked with a frown but didn't speak.

"Do you have any idea why I have this open-door policy for the uninvited looking for closure to an unsettled situation?"

"No!" And he faded away.

I gave Barney a toe nudge. "Come on, buddy, we have to find Viv again." His sad eyes seem to say, "It's about time."

We made our way back around the circular hedge, and there she was facing in the opposite direction, which allowed us to approach her from behind, once more enabling me to view her sketch.

I spoke. "You have the lake, gazebo, and roses all in your picture. That's not the way of it."

She turned toward me and closed her art pad with a *snap*! She began gathering up her supplies. "Artistic licence. I can draw whatever I want and put it wherever I want. I do not need unsolicited advice or your opinion."

I considered myself told off. I needed to make her like me and trust me a little if she was going to give me the key to her Nottawa house, but she didn't know that yet.

Before she could gather all her stuff and stow it in her bag, I blathered forth once more. "Do you come here often?"

She stopped and gave me a withering look that expressed concern for the stupid. "Is that the best line you have? Go away from this place!"

Gadzooks! She thought I was coming on to her. Well, I certainly cemented that notion out of her head, by adding, "Maybe I will see you here next Saturday then."

I must confess I waited in anticipation for Saturday to roll around. She was a young damsel in distress, and I was suppose to save the day. Who was I kidding? She was just a young college student. My interest lay more in having free rein in a house from the forties, untouched since the seventies. My collectible DNA genes were humming in full vibration. I had to rely on the ghostly vibes to make the transfer of the house key become a reality, as I had no intention of a break-and-enter scenario. My reputation was at stake, and I would be at risk of losing custody of Barney.

I googled Nottawa and was delighted to find it was sitting near the toe of Georgian Bay, an interesting part of the province I hadn't explored in many a moon. I could combine the opportunity to search the Viv house and make a scenic drive and tour of the Blue Mountain area. Barney would love the parks. It was no further than my weekend drives to Muskoka. I would just veer off to the west.

Saturday noon found me trying to stroll and look in all directions as Barney pulled me along through the gardens. There was more foot traffic on this bright, sunny day, so I had to hold him on a tighter leash. As we rounded the hedge, we spotted Viv sitting at her spot. Instead of her drawing pad, she had her camera as her tool. She turned toward us, the camera whirling. *Is that a good thing or a bad thing?* I wondered. *Is she getting proof of a stalker?*

I approached, stood near her, and waited. She spoke.

"What's your dog's name?"

"Barney. He's a purebred basset hound. He loves parks. We're going up to Collingwood and Blue Mountain next weekend. Lots of parks up there. Do you know the area?" I do motormouth at times, but there, I got it all out.

She didn't respond. I walked on pulling Barney, who suddenly seemed reluctant to move. I do believe he fancied himself photogenic.

Half a circular hedge away, I heard her speak. "Hey there, Barney's human."

I turned slowly, feigning little interest. "Yes?"

"Can I ask you something?"

"Yes?"

"Could you come back?"

I waited.

"Please?"

I went back feeling in control of the situation, at least for the moment. I waited.

"I wonder if you could do me a favour when you're up near Collingwood?"

I could think of several smart-ass remarks to counter that, but the force was with me and my mouth only because Barney tangled his human's feet on his leash.

She carried on. "My family's old house is not far from there. It is mine now, but it is still tied up in legalese. I wonder if I could persuade you to drive by and have a quick look at it. Just to make sure things are okay, you know? Hopefully, no one has broken windows or doors or stolen anything. I would pay you for your time."

"You don't know me. How do you know I can be trusted? Maybe I would break a window or door or steal something or want an outrageous payment for my time."

"Barney wouldn't let you." She looked down lovingly at my sidekick, who quickly seemed to be changing loyalties. "Would you, Barney?" Barney's reaction was just plain sloppy. Who was in control here?

"I don't even know your name, or where your house is. How would I get in, and how would I even know if something was amiss?"

"My name is Vivian Avery. My house is in Nottawa. That is a village just south of Collingwood on Highway 124. The address is 12 Turl Street, in the south part of town. Not many houses there. Small houses on big lots. Had to have room for the septic tanks when they were built in those days. It's a green slate house with a pointed roof on the front vestibule. You know, the kind they built after the Second World War?"

"And how do I get into this green slate house with the pointed roof on the front vestibule?" It seemed she needed a bit of a prod.

"I have the key right here." She dove into the carryall at her feet. Barney's nose and ears went with her. "I keep it on my key chain. Not sure why. I haven't been up to the house since last fall."

She worried over the stubborn key ring until she was able to free the selected key by going around and around the ring until it reached the end of the cycle. It was indeed an old key, well worn with the brass showing through on the active parts.

"Are you sure this key still works? It looks pretty worn."

"Worked just fine last time I used it." That seemed to be the only verification she intended to give on the subject. "Let me know if it looks like anything has been damaged or taken. Nothing is to be removed until my lawyer can sort out the legal stuff."

─────

'Twas a dark and gloomy morning when I struck out north on Highway 400. The windshield wipers were beating a slow rhythm, as was Barney's tail, but mornings were never his best time. As I made the turn and followed Highway 26 up to the Nottawasaga sideroad, the sky opened up and gave way with large raindrops splattering down, accompanied by booms of thunder and bolts of lightning. Barney covered his ears. I continued and turned north on Highway 124 to approach Nottawa from the south and followed the GPS to Turl Street.

Luck was a lady as the storm subsided and little pieces of sunshine dappled their way through the overhanging grey. As the GPS announced in her British accent that we had reached our destination, there was a wondrous sight to behold. Right before my eyes, under a double rainbow, sat a small sturdy green slate house on a big lot, with lots of room for a septic tank that houses from those days had, as I was told. This house also had a pointed roof on the front vestibule—you know, the kind they built after the Second World War?

I gazed for a few moments. A double rainbow is an awesome sight, and one must always pay homage when privileged to observe.

The driveway was not paved, and with neglect, it had become no more than two hard dirt runner trails, beckoning a vehicle forward to a lopsided one-door garage that once had a coat of white paint. The downpour had left deep wells of slurry along its route. My city-born SUV did not like the bumping and bruising as I nursed it over the long path. The overgrowth down the middle of the two tracks swept along its undercarriage with swishes and thunks.

I came to a stop in front of the old garage, with the house on my right. I gave it a visual once-over as I shut down the engine. The cement walk leading to the front door was broken and torn. Many weeds had struggled their way through the seams. A group of dandelions or two waved a greeting. The wrought iron railing around the small stoop had peeled and rusted. There was a side door that had one cement patio stone in front of it and what remained of an overhanging light. This would have made an easy entrance to and from the garage in the days of Avery residents.

My visual detecting was interrupted by Barney's whine, informing me it would be a pleasure for him to meander amongst the field of country growth. We made a tour around the small house through the long wet grass. The sun was shining on the wet, making clinging raindrops sparkle in their splendour. Birds were beginning to call and flit across the bramble branches that surrounded the old garage. No windows were broken; no damage was noted. Where to begin looking for a hidden stash was a daunting task. I had not considered the addition of an old beat-up garage. I would have to adopt the mindset of a miserly old man who liked to have nearby access to his hoard to let his fingers do the walking.

I rounded the far corner of the house and approached the three cement steps leading up to the front entrance. The old aluminum screen door screeched and scraped in reluctance as I applied force to open it. After I wiggled and jiggled the key in the lock, the wooden door creaked inward and I stepped forward, pulling a not-so-eager Barney after me.

All was still and stuffy. The vestibule was barely large enough to hold two medium-sized people if they stood one behind the other. Straight ahead, high on the wall, was a diamond-shaped mirror with fluted edges. Above the mirror, attached to the ceiling, hung a horizontal bar holding a trio of wire coat hangers sans coats. Two steps to the left took me into a small living room with four walls papered with a faded gold fleur-de-lis design that could be seen peeking out between a multitude of pictures in frames. Some of them were paint-by-numbers.

Untouched since the seventies was an understatement. A speckled gold couch, gliding beige La-Z-Boy with footstool (both loaded with cushions covered in crocheted covers), a long stereo system, one tall and two short lamps on coffee tables, and a dining table set were all squeezed together on an orange shag rug. Through it all was a well-worn trail one could follow to walk through the room to the right side of the far wall to a short hall. One could stand there and see a tiny kitchen and look into a bedroom on the left that was completely taken up by a twin bed with a coil-spring mattress. Another room on the right held a double bed; no room for anything else other than a small dresser and cupboard.

The old man must have been quite a smoker in his day as the stale odour still lingered. Every room contained ashtrays. I spied a square blue enamel one with indents at each corner to hold burning cigarettes. It had rust damage but the advertising for Wally's Diner could still be read. Another gave the phone number for Gus's Garage. Four numbers started with CH5. The pièce de résistance was a floor stand ashtray beside the La-Z-Boy. It was silver in colour and stood on a pedestal about seventy-five centimetres in height. A large round amber glass ashtray graced the top. Arcing the ashtray looped a handle engraved with a scene of a cloudy sky and an airplane flying over a tree-filled countryside. A large stand-alone moulded airplane, half the size of the ashtray, was attached to the side of the handle. It reminded me of the Avro plane that was Canada's pride and joy in days gone by. The bottom of the stand was a little lopsided and corroded. I recognized these pieces of memorabilia would be appealing in several areas of the collectible market today. They alone might tide Viv over for a few creditors.

I visually scoured the living room first. Money was flat. I had heard that people sometimes hid flat treasures behind picture frames. He would have good access to them there. People were known to tape things to the bottom of drawers, under couches, chairs, and beds. What was it his ghostly son said about that Opry singer? No, as I looked around, there was no fireplace there. *Think like a mean old man*, I thought.

I closed my eyes and put myself in the place of a mean old man wondering where to hide my loot. I never learn—that was an invitation for the mean old man himself in spirit form to announce his arrival loud and clear. He tried for intimidation.

"Who in the tarnation are you? You're trespassing! Get out of my house! Now!"

He swarmed forward and around me. He knew he could not touch me without my permission, but his icy wind sent shivers and goosebumps throughout my person. Barney growled his best growl but planted himself low, firmly between my feet.

Mean spirit took a stance a little more than a metre in front of me, with arms folded. Perhaps he was trying for the image of a genie from a lamp, but his unshaven chin covered in the residue of chewing tobacco threw a disclaimer into that picture.

"Not your house anymore. It belongs to your granddaughter Viv, and she gave me her key and asked me to come and check to make sure things are okay. See?"

I retrieved the key from my back pocket and dangled it up for him to check out as if that would make any difference.

He whirled across the room, and without warning, the blue enamel ashtray advertising Wally's Diner came hurtling forward directly in line with my head. My head managed to move to the side in time to avoid a collision. The ashtray did make contact, however, with the airplane sitting on top of the free-standing ashtray. The airplane did a solo flight as it went crashing to the floor amid the sounds of a howling basset hound.

Above the din from the direction of the front door came the voice of a living person. "Hello in there!" The door scraped open. Barney stopped howling, and we both stared at a man who stared right back.

"Hi, I'm Ray, the neighbour from down the road. Saw your wagon out front and thought I'd stop by to see if everything was okay." He gave the place a quick visual inspection, right through the middle of Grumpy Grandpa.

"Pleased to meet you, Ray, neighbour from down the road." He was not aware of how truly I meant that. "I am a friend of Viv's. She gave me her key." Once more, I dangled it forth. "I'm on my way to Blue Mountain, so she asked me to stop off and check things out."

"Oh, Viv. I remember her when she was a little kid. Sorry, I was, to hear about her dad passing away. Hope she's doing okay. Is she hanging on without selling soon? Most of us have good acreage and are waiting for a Collingwood subdivision to grow south. Well, I'll be off. Say hi to Viv from Ray, the neighbour down the road."

The screen door scraped once more as he exited the way he had entered. Spirit Grandpa had exited as well, and that was a wonderful thing too.

"Okay, Barney, where to begin." I knew I had to be careful and not let my mind wander or Mean-Spirit Grandpa would take the opportunity to bounce forth once more to harass me. There were so many places one could hide a money stash, places that would afford easy access whenever the urge to play with his loot became too great to ignore. I started with picture frames and moved on to the couch seats and cushions. By the time I had emptied and overturned closets and drawers, I found myself as dirty as a dustman and surrounded in a mire that would put a hoarder to shame.

I had run out of places to investigate, and my mindset was to lock up and head northwest to the Blue Mountain area, find a hotel, clean up, and take a scenic walk along the south shore of Georgian Bay with Barney. Tomorrow, I would return and try again. With dread, I thought about what the old garage may have to offer. Spiders and varmints and snakes, oh my!

I looked around to find Barney to see if he would agree with my plan, only to be horrified to spy him with a leg cocked relieving himself on the pedestal of the still-overturned aviator ashtray.

"Argh, Barney, stop that!" Of course, there is no stopping one until one is relieved, is there? I couldn't blame Barney. I had ignored him in his time of need.

I gingerly picked up the monstrosity, noting that the amber ashtray had not broken, although both the top and bottom fixtures were dangling from each end of the pedestal. Looking at this item was my downfall. I broke my agreement with my Avery ghost and Viv and decided to take it with me, get it fixed, bargain a price for it on the way home at the 400 Antique Market, and hope it would bring a little in the way of compensation for Viv. The end would justify the means, I told myself.

I backed out using my elbow to open the screen door, as both hands were needed to carry the wobbling parts. Barney was right with me. He had no intention of staying in the house without my protection. Quite a guard dog, he was. I placed the item in the back of my SUV, went back, locked the door, and drove away, feeling itchy and grubby.

It wasn't until the next morning I felt inclined to deal with the broken Avro, as I had so aptly named the ashtray's airplane. I donned fresh clothes, left my overnight stay, grabbed a Tim Hortons breakfast, and headed for the local Home Hardware to purchase soft cloths, rust remover, silver polish, and a spray water bottle. I picked up plenty of advertising newspapers at the exit door. I kept a set of handyman tools in my vehicle, thinking, someday, I may have to be a handyman. That day had arrived. Perhaps I could do some fixing on Avro before turning it over for a professional completion.

There are parks aplenty in our province of "A Place to Grow", As I neared Collingwood, I turned into a small roadside area. The one-way-only drive wound down to and along a shallow, rippling creek. Dotted along the way were several wooden picnic tables, each one private from the other. I chose one in the middle and pulled in beside it. Barney approved, so we took a short walk along the creek before settling down to the work at hand. I had to leave enough time to do another search at the little green house. I knew I was procrastinating and telling myself I wasn't afraid of the big bad spirit.

I tied Barney's leash to the table leg, hoisted Avro and parts out of the back of my SUV, and laid them on the picnic table, which I had covered thoroughly with newspapers, as I expected there would be some mess. I looked at the pieces. There were four parts in all hanging loose beside the Avro plane itself: the top circular piece where the amber glass ashtray sat, the handle, the pedestal, and the base. From my inspection, it appeared all pieces were screwed together, except for Avro; it was held in a holding pattern on the handle by a flat-head screw hidden under the bottom. That seemed simple enough, even for an amateur handyman.

So, where to start? Take the sections apart, wash down the pedestal, and clean off the rust from the ends, then do the same on the top and bottom. Twist it all back together. How difficult could that be?

I collected some creek water in my spray water bottle and began washing down the wet, stinking pedestal. As I worked on the rusty end, I noticed the inside had a roll of paper in it. I held it up, much like you would a telescope, but all I could see was the curled end of a paper roll, and all I got was rusty water spouting out toward me. There was just enough room to allow me to insert one forefinger knuckle deep to feel the edges of the roll. My finger emerged rusty and wet. I telescoped the pedestal once more and slowly placed it on the table. *By Jove, I think I've found it!*

I picked it up once more, turned it around, and explored the inside of the other end. The edges of soggy paper slowly unstuck under my fingernail.

I opened the passenger door of the car and withdrew my flashlight from the front compartment. When did the government, in its wisdom, stop printing paper money? We went polymer about ten years ago or so, I think.

Shining the light and flipping the edges as best I could, I was able to identify old paper money and occasionally numbers of one and zero. The pedestal was a hollow sixty-centimetre tube that appeared to be packed tightly with bills. By now, I was confident this was the old man's stash, and it seemed to be plentiful. Now, how to get it out?

There was not enough room to grab, push, or pull. I tried pushing with the handle of my screwdriver but realized there was some mushing going on. The wet bills were collapsing. Thoughts of the ghost father's story about

Stringbean Akeman's stash deteriorating and being useless sounded a warning bell. I had to give some serious thought to this removal.

Serious thought led me to think about tin cutters. With care, I could cut up the sixty-centimetre length and extract the rolls, then dry them out before unrolling them. It would ruin the piece, but no one would miss it or even know about it. Once more, I tried to convince myself the end justifies the means. Avro would still be intact. It could be returned to the little green house, along with the top section of the ashtray.

While this serious thought was churning about in the recesses of my mind, the noise of an approaching vehicle brought into view the black-and-white cruiser of one of Ontario's finest.

He rolled down his window. "Good afternoon." *Was it that time already?* "What are you doing?"

Stick as close to the truth as possible. Be sure the cops will find you out. "I'm trying to fix this old ashtray stand for a friend who likes this sort of thing."

"That is a picnic table, not a workshop bench."

"Yes, of course, Officer, sorry, you're right. Just thought I could fix it before I saw her. I'll clean up my mess and get out of here." Home free? Not so fast.

He scanned the situation with a practiced eye I knew so well from my professional assignments. My license plate gave him a clue. "You're from the city. Visiting for a few days?"

"Yes. Lovely part of our province, glad to be here, but heading back now." A little polite butter never hurts.

"What is that anyway?" With that, Officer Curious opened his door, stepped out, and approached my workbench. He had left the door open and the patrol car running—my tax dollars at work. He leaned over the attached bench and looked at the disarray, finally picking up Avro.

"This is cool. Where does it go?"

"It sits on the handle that sits on the top of the pedestal, which sits on the base." I still had a firm grip on the pedestal, although sweaty palms don't do that well.

I suppose he meant well, but I was hoping he would leave well enough alone. His interest peaked; he surveyed the parts and held his hand out for the pedestal while still mentally putting Humpty Dumpty together again.

"It's okay," I managed. "I'll pack it all up and fix it when I get home to my proper workbench. You're on duty. Don't want to take your time. Appreciate it anyway."

"Where'd you get this? I remember one like this when I was a kid. One of my buddies in Nottawa had one in his house. His dad said it was one of a kind."

He reached and took the piece out of my hand. My mind was racing with useless escape plans. If I grabbed my stuff and made a dash for it, there was no doubt I could not outrun the long arm of the law. What choice did I have? What truth could be stretched?

"Don't let him take it!" screamed Ghost Avery, who had suddenly appeared on the left side of me. "That's Ray's son, Joey. He'll know you stole it. He used to love to pretend to fly that plane when he would come over to visit!"

He swirled around the table, around Ray's son, Joey, and Barney, causing Barney to react by backing up and putting his nose up, ears waving and his whole self shivering.

Officer Joey inspected the pedestal much as I had. "That's gotta be from the old Avery house. How'd you come by it? The house has been locked up for years. I think I'd better see your ID."

While I was considering a full confession, or as close to the truth a lie can get, he continued, "There's paper wadded up in it. Is that what you were trying to get out with your screwdriver? Need something longer. I'll see what I have in the cruiser. Meanwhile, you stay put. I need to know how you got into my friend's house and why you confiscated this particular item. When the Avery items go to auction, I want this! Legally!"

I was doomed! He, no doubt, had a long-wired Taser in his cruiser, too, for runaways. Barney had been considering the dark blue pant leg and shiny black boot nearest to him with too much interest. *Oh, no, Barney, don't even think about it.*

Officer Joey looked down at Barney, gave a smile, and bent down to grace him with an ear scratch. Several things happened in an eye-blink sequence. Barney took that moment to howl his best basset howl and run between Joey's boots. Barney likes to be between feet. To keep from falling, Officer Joey reached for the table, throwing the pedestal over the side. I made a spectacular touchdown interception. Ghost Avery appeared very agitated.

"Keep him busy. I'll use my icy coolness. Not an easy thing to do."

He swished over to the cruiser and disappeared inside. He wrapped his ghostly coldness around all the electronic apparatus. It bellowed forth with a loud electric crackle that no dignified gadgetry should spew forth. The startled officer untangled his feet in tune with Barney's baying and bolted toward his vehicle. At the same time, travellers in two cars waiting in line to get past the black-and-white took it upon themselves to screech at him about his malfunctioning equipment warning him that something must be dreadfully wrong somewhere. My ghost pal was vaporized by an electric bolt. It appeared he had exploded the limits of his ghostly power by screwing up the computer system in the cruiser.

Barney and I stood and watched a private episode of comic bedlam play out before our very eyes. Our officer banged and ill-treated his computer while trying to reach his dispatcher. The people behind him had exited their vehicles and were recording him on their cells for posterity. When he realized their intentions and understood he may end up going viral in an unbecoming way, he geared up and, in a flurry of dust and small pebbles, roared off for parts unknown. The spectators were left with a "nothing to see here, folks," look in their eyes, so without further ado, they carried on their way too.

I was left with Barney and our ashtray mess just as we had been before, in our not too distant past. All was quiet in the park, except for twittering birds and scampering squirrels that appeared to be taunting me. I gathered up all the bits and pieces, stowed them in a green garbage bag, and made a hasty exit.

I drove down Highway 114, keeping my speed at five kilometres over the limit, as that would raise no red flags. Serious thought came upon me once more. I could get tin cutters at the Home Hardware but I had left that store behind me. No doubt there would be some in the ramble shack garage at the Avery house. I expected mean spirit Grandfather would be standing guard there though, if I wasn't careful. Oh, what to do! What to do!

Serious thought number two light-bulbed its way forward. The wet rolls would be puffy and take up room. If they were dry, they would shrink and be loose. It was worth a try to dry them while still inside, somehow.

Serious thought number three: How? A hairdryer!

After buying said item and lots of batteries in Nottawa, I found a busy parking lot at a strip mall and tried my best to blend in with the rest of the vehicles. I blew hot air up, down, in, and out of the pedestal tube for more time than I was aware of. Each time I checked my progress, I was rewarded with a little more waving of the edges of the rolls. Finally, with care and bated breath, I inserted tweezers and slowly pulled first on one edge, then on another. The roll nudged a centimetre toward me. A little more heat, then a little more coaxing. Finally, I had enough of the roll to hold and twist the way it was folded. It had been held with an elastic band that had completely deteriorated. When I had a complete roll out, the dry end opened on its own. I set it aside, not wanting to rush, even though I was as anxious as I reckon old Grandpa must have been to tally it up.

    I pointed the hairdryer up the other end to continue the slow but productive process. Time passed. Store doors clicked closed. The parking spots around me became vacant. I stuck out like a sore thumb. I could stay no longer for fear of Ray the neighbour's son, Officer Joey, finding me. I extracted a total of six rolls. Some were bound more tightly than others. I did indeed feel like Scrooge McDuck, wanting to revel in the counting of the stash.

    Caring for all six as one might care for fresh eggs, I set them on the passenger side floor, giving them room to air. I intended to make sure they were bone dry before easing them open and ironing them straight. Would that work? I had no legitimate nor illegitimate persons to solicit for advice upon the matter. Meanwhile, the ashtray stand and Avro needed my attention. If I could fix it, it could be returned to the house. No need now to take it to the antique market.

    I have been in more detective jams while detecting and have been able to detect solutions. I have learned to face the music and hide in plain sight while staying calm and cool. Having a believable story with a B and C backup plan on hand is essential, so, I drove on to 12 Turl Street.

Plan A was to drive around to the back of the house, where Ray, the neighbour down the road, would not see me, sit in the hatchback, and make the broken whole. If I kept my mind on the task with all the business I could muster, perhaps Grandpa Spirit would not find the weak link in my aura.

It went well. So well, I was suspicious. Had fortune finally smiled down upon me? Looping Barney's leash over my left wrist, I held the amber glass tray while I clasped the now-secure pedestal by my right hand. Avro was indeed taken for a flight as we rounded the corner of the house and up the three cement steps. The ashtray remained steady as I set it down to scrape open the aluminum screen door once more, inserted the key, and entered. The stale, musty tobacco smell hit me in the face again. With guilt, I surveyed the mess I had made while looking for the stash. After setting the ashtray in its designated spot, it behooved me to straighten things up a little. I began by hanging up the pictures, then proceeded to tidy up the cushions and pillows. I was adjusting the drawers and cupboards when Barney's backward shuffle toward my feet and his growls alerted me to the cold draft expelled in my direction by the spirit of the former owner of the property. I turned my head toward him.

"You made a mess, and now in cleaning it up, you have overstayed your welcome." He sneered at me while he thrust his chin up and down in the direction of the front window. "I'm gonna have fun watching this and seeing you in handcuffs. That's what happens to thieves in Nottawa. We raise our own lawmen here."

I looked out the window at the sound of Nottawa's own slamming the door of his black-and-white. Barney crouched lower. Officer Joey approached the steps cautiously, right hand palming the butt of his holster. I froze. He stood to the side of the open door and shouted, "Hello? This is the police. Who's in there? Identify yourself!"

Barney identified himself before I had a chance to. He gave his basset hound bay in his best low tenor. Spirit Grandpa was gleefully sticking around, hoping for a devastating outcome.

Our brave Ontario Provincial policeman stuck his head around the edge of the door and appeared visibly relieved when he recognized Barney and me rather than an actual threat. This allowed him to become very brave.

"You again? What's going on? Are you armed? Put your hands in front of you, where I can see them. Come out of there."

Three questions and two directions at once was a challenge, so when in doubt, answer a question with a question.

"Look, the Avro airplane ashtray is still here. Can you see it? I fixed it. It looks good, don't you think?"

He moved further into the vestibule and shifted his gaze over to where he knew the sliding armchair and ashtray would be. He then looked at me with question marks in his eyes.

Spirit Grandpa thought he was entitled to take it upon himself to lay back in his favourite chair and place his misty feet on the footstool. He looked like he was smoking.

I rambled on. "You were correct. It is one of a kind. It was broken, as you know. I took it upon myself to take it and fix it. I have the key to the house, as you can also see." I held it up in view, taking the chance he wouldn't unholster his firearm when I lowered my hand to the back packet of my jeans to get it.

His interest zipped from me to the Avro. It took him three boot thumps to reach it. He placed one knee on the footstool, his actual knee going through the non-actual feet of

Grandpa. Grandpa pulled back and turned to flip out of the chair, screaming aloud, "Bugger!" But only I could hear.

Our officer placed his hands on the arc handle and Avro. He gave a memory smile as he smoothed his hands over it. He shuddered. "It's cold in here, and it stinks." He grasped the handle with both hands and raised the whole thing high for a better look. "I don't think little Viv would care or even miss this if I took it home for safekeeping, do you?"

He gave me a look that indicated I had better agree or I could be followed all the way back to Toronto. Before I could respond, Spirit Grandpa showed his disappointment at the homegrown law enforcement.

"Leave it be, you young scallywag. You haven't changed at all, have you? What a disgrace you are to us all."

He wafted over to the side table and picked up and once more threw the blue enamel Wally's Diner ashtray disc-like across the room. It made contact with the official OPP cap perched on Joey's head, which then took an airborne flight. Grandpa made a frantic figure-eight swirl around the officer and ashtray stand.

Barney and I became a captive audience. Officer Joey turned as pale as Grandpa. With a wide-eyed, open-mouthed look, he gradually became knowledgeable.

"I think old man Avery is still here." With that, he dropped the ashtray with no regard to Avro's nosedive, moonwalked backwards, and made a scurried exit.

Have you ever heard a spirit cackle? Grandpa was over the top with revengefulness. How he was enjoying the flight. I didn't care, nor did Barney. We raised our heads in dignity and, with a sure-footed march, made our way out the door, locked it, shut the aluminum screen with a final screech, trudged our way around the side from whence we came, got into our getaway car, and lit out. The tiny prick of taillights of the cruiser could faintly be seen in the distance.

Call me Scrooge McDuck, but it was rather fun ironing out old bills. Laying them flat, sorting, and counting took some delightful time. Some rolls held more than others. Some were fifty denominations, most were hundreds. When all was sorted and counted, the grand total was fifty thousand, with the possibility that a few were valuable. This was a neat little nest egg that Grandpa was reluctantly passing on.

"No one needs to know about it, so it can be called hush money," Ghostly Father told me at our next gazebo encounter. He was tickled pink to hear my bill rescue tale but somewhat saddened by my spirit story. "Tell her whatever story you wish to concoct, but be kind. She has enough on her plate. She doesn't need a guilt trip."

"Kind, I can be. But payment, I need," I persisted.

"I know, I haven't forgotten. I told you Viv would give you payment."

"I refuse monetary payment. I don't want any part of that money." I was getting a little annoyed.

"For a detective, you are not detecting all that well!" He was even more annoyed. "Give her the stash, get your reward, and stop bothering me."

With a shiver and a shake, he was gone. It seemed he was more injured, insulted, and arrogant than I was.

Barney and I had to do a little scouting, as Viv was not in her usual spot. I was carrying her stash in my backpack. Awareness of its contents made it very heavy and made me mindful of suspicious minds that may give more than one glance in my direction. We wandered down the path leading to the stone archway, past the unique tree without a centre growth. We spotted her in a new location. The sun was shining through the trees, leaving a dappled pattern on the terra firma. She was prettier than the picture she was sketching. It was a charcoal outline of the brick wall with forsythia hanging every which way. It was Barney who gave us away. He gave his "hi there" woof that she seemed to recognize immediately. She flipped her head around, causing a cascade of brown hair to spill over her shoulder.

"Hi, Barney, have you brought your human here to give me good news or bad news?"

I waited.

"Well?" she finally inquired.

"Oh. Are you talking to me? I was solidly under the impression you were addressing Barney."

She ignored that completely and gave a snobby sniff.

"Scooch over," I told her. I sat beside her and filled her in on the state of her house. It was fine, I told her. It was just waiting for her to take possession and do with it what she wished. Leaving out all the bits, I took the stash out of my backpack. I had packaged the money in several cloth grocery bags. I presented her with them after telling her the find was legitimate. There were no questions to be asked nor answered, and she must leave it at that. Amen!

To my delight, she was not surprised. She took the packages and set them on the bench on the other side of her. After all my care and concern, she seemed rather nonchalant about the whole thing, but then I had left out all the bits and asked for no questions or answers.

She made no effort to peek inside. She was no curious cat.

"Thank you," she finally said. "My father told me Grandpa used to hide his money away in places around the house. Sometimes, Dad would find it, but it was never there when he looked again, as Grandpa kept moving it. It was like a game to him. I am sure it will be a big help to me now."

"You're welcome." I got up to leave after having to coax Barney to come with me. Fickle fellow.

"Oh, by the way."

"Yes?"

"How was your holiday in the Blue Mountains?"

"Fine, just fine. Uneventful." I turned to leave once more.

"Before you go."

"Yes?" She had me twirling around Barney's leash.

"Could I have my key back, please?"

"Of course, sorry." I fished it out of my jeans' back pocket and stepped back to her. She reached for it and gave another thank-you.

I turned and slowly moved away once more. Sometimes, you just have to wait for it.

"I'm sorry." She raised her voice to get my attention. "Please come back. I have something for you."

Aha! Would it be something in that carryall that I should feign uninterested in and not peek inside when she presented it? I returned.

She dove into her large flowered bag that always seemed to be beside her feet and drew out two packages approximately ten by sixteen inches, both wrapped loosely in white tissue paper. Needless to say, they were pictures.

Patience thy name may be Viv, but it is not mine. I needed to see them right away. I sat down again. Barney proceeded to happily lie down between my feet. I placed both packages on my lap and unwrapped one.

I now understood what Viv meant by artistic licence. There it was. She had captured all of the gardens in one fell swoop, and in the middle was Barney and his human. We were on the walkway leaving the gazebo. We were surrounded by the beauty of the rose gardens, hedges, and the flowing branches of trees and bushes caught in the breezes from the lake beyond the bluffs. It was done in shades and fades of watercolour. It truly displayed her talent. I looked over at her and smiled. She nodded her thanks. I wrapped it up again and placed it under the second one. I then opened that one.

Barney was perfection in a black-and-grey charcoal sketch! An exact likeness, it was, right down to the two freckles on his nose. His head was resting on the ground. His front paws were on top of his floppy ears, which crinkled down beside his jowls and spilled out to the ground. His eyes, so sad, sleepy, and bored, were looking upward. On each side of him, from the ground up, were my dirty white sneakers, with unruly tied laces, jeaned lower legs, and knobby knees. She had signed it and named it: *Barney and His Human*. I was speechless. I could not look at her.

I wrapped it back up. "It was worth the errand," I told her. "Best of luck going forward."

Barney sensed it was time to say, "The end." He wagged goodbye.

6 THE CASE OF THE CUDDLING CAT

IT SOUNDED LIKE A pleasant assignment when CODA presented me with the paperwork for the unbalancing inventory in a quaint country store near the village of Port Perry. The balance sheet showed a discrepancy between the items sold and the incoming monetary gain. The owner, I read, was quite perplexed. He had checked and rechecked and was unable to detect the reason for this.

He had the latest electronic equipment installed both inside and outside of his establishment, and nothing seemed amiss. His staff attended to their chores in good order and were alert to any unusual activities of a person or persons taking advantage of the open displays in this wonderful country setting. The accounting showed the discrepancy was happening in little bits on a daily or weekly basis. It amounted to one hundred dollars or so, at a time. Not enough to raise a red flag immediately, but eventually, a pattern emerged. The loss started to take its toll as last year drew to a close and the Christmas rush had ended. When tax time raised its annual ugly head, it became apparent the discrepancy ballooned into quite a large amount for a small business when it surfaced in the loss column. The red ink was a worrisome amount. Ed, the shopkeeper, surmised the total damage for December alone amounted to approximately five thousand dollars.

This nagged Ed on many levels. The burn of his ulcer could no longer be quenched by a tablet or two. He was an honest, church-going Christian family man who believed in spreading kindness and goodness to all mankind. All mankind, then, would surely love the Lord and give kindness and goodness back to Ed and never would think of stealing from him. So it was that doubts were causing clouds to form in his belief.

His country store hearkened back to the days of yore when life was simple, or so Ed dreamed. He held a vision of what a general store here many years ago, in a small community on a hill called Raglin, would be like. He checked old photos, decided what goods he should stack, and hoisted up a large sign that proclaimed his store as "Yore Store."

A full-length covered veranda with two long plank steps took customers up to the solid oak door of Ed's Yore Store. Ed proudly displayed an ornate oak door with a large leaded pane glass insert that allowed his staff to see who was about to enter so they could call a greeting to them cheerfully and by name if they knew it. An old screen door replaced it during the summer months. There was a tinkling bell that dangled over the threshold announcing every entry. The flooring had been purchased from an old barn demolition, so it was well-worn and added to the charm with its creaks and groans as one approached the long counter that stretched down one side of the front room. The building was partitioned into many rooms. Each room was a unique department featuring selected wares.

The front room held the fruit, vegetables, and country-fare home baking. One could wander through the rooms, deciding where to stop and shop at leisure. Clothing, shoes, hardware, gifts, linens, or sports. One-stop shopping was not the modern-day rat race in stores we have come to know as marts.

The hidden electronic eyes and sweeping cameras were always at work and never noticed by the contented customers, but still, the balance sheets were unbalanced.

Ed felt an added insult to injury. It was time to take action and call in professionals to do their professional detection. Hence came I to save the day.

A couple of pleasant days were spent with Ed as he gave me a tour around his Yore Store inside and out. I asked him not to introduce me to his employees but to show me around on the pretence I was sizing the place up to give him an estimate on upgrades and painting. According to Ed, he and his staff were one big happy family. They would never do a dastardly deed like cheating on him, but he accepted my request reluctantly. I observed his staff did work well together. The clientele consisted of travellers passing through on their way to other destinations, while others made Yore a regular stop. I watched and prepared notes on the consistent behaviours of the peculiarities of these shoppers. Nothing appeared amiss in the business being conducted in Yore Store.

After a week of watching for nefarious activities, it was time to meet Ed with my first report.

We met for lunch in one of the many wonderful Brock Street restaurants Port Perry has to offer. Reluctantly, I handed Ed my hard copy report and informed him I was no closer to solving his mystery than when I first took his case. All merchandise had been stocked, shelved, and itemized correctly. A customer purchased, and the salesclerk scanned and entered the purchase without error. Credit cards were itemized with perfection, yet there it was. At the end of the week, we were faced with another discrepancy, and in all my wisdom and experience, I had no clue.

As per his agreement with CODA, I informed Ed he had the option of continuing weekly or being completely refunded. Ed took a large bite of his Scugog special sandwich and chewed thoughtfully for an overabundant amount of time. He then set the remainder of his sandwich on his plate, shoved it aside, folded his arms on the table, leaned forward, looked me squarely in the eye, and gave me his decision.

"Well, Daniel, you've put in a good week's worth of work; I've watched you. You've not shirked your duty in the least. I'm prepared to give it a little more time. If I let you go, I'm still in my muddle, aren't I? Proceed, if you will."

I thanked him and informed him I would try to look at the dilemma from an entirely different point of view. I didn't inform him of the disadvantage of having a report of a failed case on my record.

Ed looked at ease after making his decision. He leaned back in the ornate wooden chair and made another announcement.

"I'll tell you what, Mr. Detective. Why don't we both take the afternoon off? Play hooky." He smiled like a naughty schoolboy. "I'd like you to come home with me and meet my wife. I'd also like to show you my home. It would give you an idea why I enjoy my store and researching the history of Port Perry and the surrounding villages back to and before our 1867 Confederation. My house is one of the oldest in Port and dates back before Port was a port."

Ed looked rather smug as he told me this. It also piqued my curiosity, as I have a fondness for seeking out Canadian history. I accepted his offer, and we left our lunch.

"We can walk," he said as we started up Brock Street. "I live just up the hill a little and one block over. You need to see the town. You can come back and pick up your car later."

As we strolled up Brock, I got a history lesson whether I wanted it or not.

"My house," he began, "sits up a little higher than the town's main street. It's not a hill but when the house was built it would have been. People kept chopping at it. The house was not large to begin with. When I did renovations, it was clear when and where additions and changes had been made and during what time period.

"The house faces down toward the lake, and its occupants would have had an excellent view of the ships and barges coming in. The railroad was built right along the edge of Lake Scugog, so tourists from Oshawa, Peterborough, and as far away as Toronto could step right off the train and be smack dab in the village.

"I can only see the lake today if I go up to what was the maid's quarters on the third floor, as many buildings are obstructing the view. The house, when built in 1863 according to the town development plan, sat alone for a few years. The original owner, a family man by the name of Patterson, owned most of the acreage around it. He gardened a good deal of the land, and eventually down the hill from his house, he built and ran a harness shop and a glassworks factory. He must have been a very enterprising man.

"The original house had three wide steps that took you up to the front door. It opened on the right side. As you entered the hallway, you were met with a large room on the left and a rising curved staircase on the right. The upstairs had three tiny bedrooms and a linen closet.

"The large front room must have been quite spectacular. It had an oversized window, which was unusual for the time, but it is surmised Patterson wanted to admire the lake view and keep in touch with the comings and goings of the town activities. This large room had a wide stone fireplace that was open on both sides, as it served the dual purpose of cooking and heating the house.

"On the other side of the fireplace was a kitchen, where the family ate their meals unless they had company; then, they would set up a table in the large room. At the back of the kitchen, Patterson built a summer room that served them in the heat of the summer months. That was their form of air conditioning. It was just slatted so the wind could blow through and give ventilation. Nailed to the wall was a set of narrow stairs that led up to a tiny room for the live-in maid. During the winter months, the maid could access her room from the upstairs hall by dropping down a tiny set of stairs at the end of the narrow hallway. The stairs were kept up along the ceiling by a rope on a hook when she was not in her room so she could use the set of inside stairs that led into the large room. The pulley and the hook are still there."

Ed smiled at me as if this piece of information was a great gift he was sharing. I smiled back when he made the universal hand gesture that indicates "you go first" when we came to the walkway leading up to an imposing red brick house with a wrap-around veranda. All woodwork was trimmed with fresh cream and green paint. Ed held me back by placing one hand on my arm. He wanted me to take in the view of his house and expound upon its glory. I did because it was easy to do so.

"It is spectacular, Ed. You have put a lot of work into it. Congratulations!"

"Yes, I have, but a few others before me have added here and changed there as it has moved along through the years. A carriage house was added on the back when automobiles became available, and a grease pit was dug in the floor with steps so work could be done on the vehicles right there. That, of course, has been modernized."

I could appreciate the gardens around the house had been placed with care and selected to blend in with the style of the Victorian-Georgian setting. As we reached the wide steps leading up to the veranda, I suddenly had to do a foot stutter as a black and white cat decided to twirl around my ankles. I managed to avoid a collision and kept pace with Ed as we proceeded up the steps. He did not seem to notice my reaction. I looked back but could not locate the object of my near disaster. That should have been my first clue.

"Come in, please." Ed was most accommodating. "Edna! We have company."

Edna appeared right on cue. Her smile and demeanour seemed to make her the perfect match for the kind Ed. She welcomed me and ushered me along into a large, well-decorated showroom and through a short, low-ceiling hall into an indoor-outdoor room that spoke of relaxation, lemonade, or beer in tall glasses.

We sat down on wicker loungers with matching cushions and plump pillows, and niceties were exchanged. I then asked my question.

"Do you have a cat?"

They both looked somewhat startled.

"No, we don't," countered Ed. "Why do you ask?"

"I just about tripped over a black and white cat as we started up your walk. Did you not notice him?" Inwardly, I was begging Ed, *Please say yes, or that he belongs to the neighbour.*

Ed and Edna exchanged knowing eye contact, and Edna spoke to him. "Tell him what happens, Ed. It won't matter what he thinks. He is a detective; he detects." She turned her delicate face toward me and graced me with a gentle smile.

"After all these years," he began, "it is hard to believe we are only the fourth owners of this house. The first was the builder, Mr. Patterson. His daughter was here for a few years after he died; then it sat empty.

"In the early 1920s, along came a prominent man about town. Mr. Downs was his name. He married and raised his family of five. His wife, Lila, was the love of his life. She was a very strict and righteous woman. She lived, as we have been told, by the Bible. Very frugal, she was, not wasting time, money, or substances. All her children did their country's duty during the war and returned to care for her in her elderly years after Mr. Downs passed away. She outlived them as well. She continued to live here in her beloved house. She did not venture upstairs in her older years. A bathroom was installed under the staircase in the tiny closet that was the cloakroom. The kitchen was turned into a bedroom, and the summer kitchen was insulated to become the main kitchen."

Ed hesitated in his telling and nodded at Edna, who quickly picked up the thread. It was obvious this was the way the story had been related to listeners before me.

"There was a young couple—the Nilsons—who built their house across the street," Edna continued. She lifted her arm and moved it in the direction of the house. "It is still there and lived in by another young couple. I had become friends with Minnie Nilson when she was older, and she told me many stories about Lila. Minnie is in residential care now, but she is still a joy to visit."

Edna stopped and put her hands on her knees with a definite purpose. "Oh, I am getting off-topic here. Back to the cat! Lila Downs had a cat called Cuddles. She doted on Cuddles. Minnie would tell me stories of how Lila inspected her backyard garden every morning with Cuddles strolling up and down the rows of rhubarb, asparagus, and beans. Cuddles would move between her feet in a rhythm only the two of them knew.

"Minnie would play dominos with Lila some evenings to help her pass the time. Cuddles would sit on the chair between them as if she was watching every move Lila made. At dinnertime, Cuddles's food dish was placed at the foot of Lila's chair so they could eat together. Lila was meticulous in her cleanliness and tidiness, so even Cuddles's dish was cleaned and put away after every meal. That cat slept with Lila too. Lila slept on her side, so Cuddles was always tucked into the small of her back, kind of keeping her from falling over."

Edna moved her hands in a rolling motion, indicating how Lila would not list or lean.

"'That ball of furriness lived for nineteen years, would you believe? When she died, Lila had a small casket made for her and she held a ceremony as she laid Cuddles to rest out in her vegetable garden between the rows of beans, where they both loved to walk. A tiny wooden cross was erected on the site. It's gone now, so is the vegetable garden."

Edna paused, and Ed took over. These two were more in sync than Lila and her Cuddles.

"Lila finally had to be moved to local residential care, where she met her demise. This house, once more, remained empty for a few years while the several grandchildren jumped through the legal hoops and managed to put it on the real-estate market. It was a down time for real estate, so it sat for a while. A young couple purchased it at a reasonable price, realizing it needed a good deal of work and restoration. The wiring needed to be replaced, the furnace was an old octopus, the roof leaked, and the wallpaper on every ceiling and wall was falling off. The beauty of the French doors leading into the dining room and the kitchen and the grand fireplace were the selling features.

"The young couple spent time, money, and energy on a modernization campaign that lasted four years before they relisted the property. The reason put forth was his company was transferring him out west. The housing market still had not recovered when Edna and I purchased it from them. We were quite delighted with our find and eager to begin the renovations and make the changes we wished.

"The neighbours made us welcome. We laughed at their references to the haunted house and live-in ghosts, as these comments were made tongue-in-cheek. A visit from the couple we purchased it from was unexpected. They came around about three months after we had settled in. We sat on the front veranda with them and enthusiastically told them of our grandiose plans. They listened, then asked if we had encountered any strange happenings. Edna and I both looked at them in wonder and shook our heads. When we asked them what they meant, they shrugged their shoulders, changed the subject, and departed shortly thereafter."

Edna once more took over the story. "That evening Ed and I held our mutual confession. We had indeed noticed just a few oddities but hadn't shared them. It seemed items we had left out were put in their proper place, and carelessly stored items were tidied up. Little food crumb messes cleaned themselves. The bedroom window curtains sometimes were found open early on a sunny morning when we were sure we had closed them the night before. During the night, there were times when it felt like something, or someone, was moving across our legs. Sometimes, I could not roll over onto my back, as it seemed something was blocking my movement."

Edna gave a little embarrassed chuckle. "I tried to blame that on Ed, but he proclaimed his innocence."

She leaned back in her tapestry lounge and gave me a "believe me or not" look. "We're convinced Lila and Cuddles are still making their presence known here. They either don't want to. or are unable to leave. We don't mind, really, do we, Ed?"

Ed gave an "if you say so" nod and picked up the tale. "It scares the living daylights out of our grandkids, though. They don't take too kindly to the happening when they find themselves being tucked into bed tightly, mysteriously, and feeling little cat paws prancing about or on them. One time, they brought their poodle with them. In the middle of the night, that poor little dog jumped off the bed, ran out into the hall, and frantically barked back into the room. His curly hair was standing up, unfurled on end, all along his back, and he never would enter that bedroom again.

"Their parents are quite concerned about these happenings as well. They're at the point of visiting us only for a few hours during bright sunny afternoons now." Ed gave a sigh. "We do miss them. Yes, we do."

We had a few moments of melancholy silence before Ed slapped his knee and loudly exclaimed, "Well!" He grabbed the arms of his chair and stood up. "I didn't bring you into our home to fill you full of tales about our resident ghost and her cat. You're much too gracious as a listener."

"Not at all," I responded truthfully, "but I really must be going. I'll enjoy my walk back downtown to my car. So lovely to meet you, Edna."

On that note, I exited through the exquisitely carved oak front door, with an oval-shaped leaded glass window. I stepped carefully down the perfectly painted green veranda steps onto the brick walk, taking extra notice where I tread. That notice was needed, as there was the black and white cat I assumed was Cuddles swishing around my ankles once more. I was aware my feet would walk right through her without a stumble nor a yelp, and they would feel a bit of a tingle, but it just didn't seem right somehow. No need to worry, as this time, he was being reprimanded.

"Cuddles, leave the young man alone! Now scoot! Scoot!"

Cuddles arched her back, held her tail high, keeping a hook on the tip, and did indeed scoot back toward the house.

This apparition could only be Mrs. Lila Downs, owner and keeper of the house and cat for more years than I have been on this planet.

She was of average height and on the thin side. Her iron-grey hair was pulled into a bun at the back of her neck. A few strands were loose and fairly danced along the sides of her well-worn worried face. She wore a flowered cotton work dress, with flower-shaped buttons done up from her neck to the bottom of the hem. It was kept in place by a matching thin cotton belt. Beige cotton stockings and sensible Oxford shoes rounded off her outfit. She reminded me of pictures I had seen of my great-granny on the family farm.

She moved briskly to my side and announced, "I'll walk along with you. I know the way much better than you, even though things have changed for the worse."

She never introduced herself. It was a given I knew who she was. She was quite spry. I had to move quickly to keep up. Thoughts of an enjoyable stroll were blown in the wind.

I waited, but not for long. My curiosity got the better of me. Her arms were bent, and her faux leather purse swung along at the crook of her elbow, which was tucked tightly against her waist, as was her other elbow, but her hands were in front of her, and they were very busy playing some sort of finger game. I had to ask.

"What are you doing? With your hands, I mean?"

"Knitting. One must not waste the time the good Lord has seen fit to give us neither here nor there."

She had a definite "do as I say" voice. One could only answer, "Yes, ma'am," and do her bidding. I witnessed even Cuddles knew that. I wondered how her five offspring were managed.

"And what is that you are holding up to your ear, young man? Do you have an earache?"

"No, ma'am," I answered most respectfully. "Passersby will think I am talking on my cellphone and not to you."

She gave me a look of noncomprehension, but that was of no concern. She jumped right into the reason for our walk.

"You seem to be the lad that can fix our problem. Ed and Edna are quite capable of looking after my house. She's a little lax at tidiness but big on cleanliness. I sometimes must pull at their ankles to get them out of bed when the sun comes up. They do like to sleep past six o'clock. I would be quite happy to leave, but Cuddles is the problem, don't you see?"

Well, no, I didn't see, so I waited.

"Cuddles is of the mind it's still her duty to care for the residents of her home and give them care, attention, and comfort. She especially adores the little ones when they visit, as they remind her of the days when she watched over my youngsters."

"That's all very well and good, ma'am, but I'm at a loss to understand how I would be the lad to fix your problem." I thought I was very clever with my response, but she cut me down much as a mother would an insubordinate offspring.

"Don't be cheeky, young man! Use the common sense God gave you. Tell them to get a cat! Once Cuddles becomes aware there is a living replacement to take over the cuddle duties, she will be quite happy to be a dearly departed."

Now this seemed too simple to be workable, but the best-laid plans usually are, aren't they? I came forth with my usual response at this time of an arrangement.

"And what will be my payment, Mrs. Downs? I assume you understand there must be one that has no monetary value."

She stopped her brisk walking and held her hands still. I was afraid, for a moment, that her payment was going to be in the form of a pair of knitted ghostly socks, but no. I was glued to the Brock Street sidewalk by a stern, disgusted look.

"Do you not do good deeds, Daniel O'Patrick, out of the goodness of your Christian heart? Must there always be a payment? Payment will come when you meet your Maker at the end of your earthy struggle. The glory of God will shine upon you, and He will have an account of all your good deeds."

The ministerial gleam in her eyes as she laid her sermon on my conscience would have put my family pastor to shame, but I was not to be deferred.

"Mrs. Downs, if word got around in the ghostly realm that I was handing out freebies or even giving a discount, I'd have a lineup at my weak aura that I would not be able to accommodate. Now let us both bow our heads, close our eyes, rest our minds, and think of a payment."

"No time to waste. I always have a backup plan. Payment will help you and poor Ed as well."

The colourful flowers on her dress were becoming colourless; I knew her strength was fading.

"Quickly then," I prodded. "I'm all ears."

"Indeed, you are." She smirked, taking a final look at my cell phone. "Stop thinking outside the box; many items are sold inside boxes."

Her fading out was not by bits and parts, as it is with some, but a gradual fading of all. Quite nicely done, I had to admit.

And there I stood on Brock Street, all alone with my cell phone at my ear, pondering the last words of the dearly beloved and deceased Lila Downs.

~~~

I decided that looking into the box situation at the Yore Store should be my priority rather than getting the Eds a cat. Even though it was close to the end of the working day, I located my car and swung south to the popular mercantile adventure. It was fairly busy when I arrived. It would be closing soon, but I needed to embed myself in the storeroom so that when the last customer was checked out, I could roam freely amongst whatever boxes I could find. Not a very fine plan, but that was as good as I could think of at the moment. I had not thought to ask Ed for a key.

As I entered the front door and heard the jangle of the welcome bell, Ed's top clerk snapped a look my way and then quickly turned his attention back to his customer. I recognized her as a regular. I also was attuned to the fact the customer was buying shoes in a box and a flashlight in a box—a simple sale. The clerk scanned the bars, took the credit card, rang up the sale precisely, and tickety-boo, no harm, no foul there. Boxes in a bag, a "see ya later," "have a good day, eh," and on to the next customer.

I made my way to the basement where Ed had his supplies stored. I browsed around a little until I was certain Yore Store was locked up tight and all was still. There were many boxes: some large, some small, some open, some not at all. Lila had been very stingy with her clues, leaving me little to detect with.

I looked about at the neatness of Ed's storage. He had everything laid out according to each room's needs. His inventory was not large, as most was kept on the customer's floor.

"Think inside the boxes," echoed in my ear, so I peeked under the lid of a shoebox sitting on top of the pile in the footwear section. It was similar to the shoe box I had observed a customer buying as I entered the store. The box contained only tissue paper and separation cardboard. *Now, why would Ed keep empty boxes in his inventory?* Spurred on with curiosity, I removed the lids of several more boxes. Some contained shoes, but many did not.

I moved on to the hardware department storage and checked inside a few more boxes. The same phenomenon occurred. On to the china, silverware, and keepsakes. By now, I was surrounded by a mess of boxes of all sizes and assortments, but few with items. The Eds would be horrified at my mess.

I sat cross-legged on top of a rather large box advertising "Lawnmower, assembly required," fired up my iPad, and checked out Ed's inventory spreadsheet. I detected some exceedingly large clues hiding in plain sight.

The biggest box I know about is called a dumpster. I felt the need to check one out. My earlier investigation showed me there were two located just outside the rear double doors. It did not take long to find my way there. As I pushed open and walked through the double doors, I heard them clang shut behind me. That did not register a warning as the decision of which dumpster to check first was a no-brainer. Sitting on top of one, calmly cleaning one white paw, sat one lonely cat—a common occurrence in any alleyway—but this one I considered with suspicion. With a struggle, I pushed upward and held the large lid of the dumpster. I looked down into the inner sanctum of scariness while holding my breath. Although the light was very dim, as only a solitary streetlight offered a beam to the back of the store, I was able to make out several boxes. I needed to secure them for further evidence if this case was to be solved. Once more, I had prevailed by wit and knowledge!

I could not reach them, nor could I hold the dumpster lid open much longer. An Oshawa Patrol car turned the corner and brightly shone its headlights on me just as I let the cover drop with a clang that could be heard with echoes. Yes, caught like a deer in the headlights, as the saying goes. That was me.

Knowledge and wit were tested when I was in handcuffs at the station, trying to explain why I was dumpster diving late at night. Who knew that was against the law?

ID? *Yes, sir, in my jacket.* Where? *In the basement of Yore Store, which is locked up tight, the doors had closed behind my exit. Yes, that's my car, Constable.* Licence? Keys? *In my jacket, in the basement.* Why was I in the basement?

Port Perry is still a town with small-town manners where most long-time residents know each other. Hence it was, the kind officer decided he was not about to wake the Eds to verify my existence, especially when I confessed they weren't aware of where I was or why.

I was given lodging for the night, courtesy of the Durham Detention Services. I may have been able to catch a wink or two, except for the fact that every time I felt a nod, I also felt a lump near my back prohibiting me from rolling over into a more comfortable position. I swear I heard soft purring amid the other ugly, unfamiliar sounds.

With the advent of dawn, Ed was notified of my dilemma, and he asked the officer in charge to deliver me back from whence I came and that he would come down and vouch for me.

I was fearful by then the dumpster would be empty, and indeed, it was. All my solid evidence was now in a landfill. I asked Ed if we could meet in his office that afternoon and I would give him my report that would solve his mystery. He seemed more amused and eager to hear the tale of my misfortune than the solution to his unbalanced books. He readily agreed.

To show the trail of complicity, I began by giving Ed a tour of his Yore Store basement. His amusement trickled away as he gradually picked up the scent of the trail. A box of china dishes could be stuffed with socks and a variety of small items lifted out of their original boxes. Those boxes were then discarded as empty and presumably sold, but a sale was never recorded. Ed, the trusting soul that he was, was hesitant to believe me, as there were no empty boxes in his storeroom to be found. Once more, I took the trail out to the dumpster.

Making sure the double doors stayed open this time, I pushed open the dumpster lid and invited Ed to hold his breath and look inside with me. The dumpsters had been emptied in the early morn, but later, one of Ed's long-time employed clerks, suspecting something was amiss, had taken the telltale boxes from storage and had thrown them into the dumpster. One black and white cat stood on the rim of the lid and looked down with us. Ed did not seem to notice. If cats have nine lives, this feline was riding the ragged edge.

It hurt the Eds more than spreadsheets can tell that a trusted clerk and three faithful customers had done him such wrong. I took the time to educate Ed on surfing online auctions and selling sites. To his dismay, he was able to identify several items that were unique to his Yore Store. A lesson learned was his motto, and he bowed his head in good grace.

"It makes me very sad." Ed seemed to wish he had never found out. "How can I ever thank you?"

"Pay your bill on time," I quipped, and executing my favourite exit, I turned back, scratched my forehead with the back of my thumb, and added, "And get a cat!"

———

I had almost forgotten about my Yore Store case, as time does move along much faster than one would want if one had their druthers. About a month later, I received a call from Edna. She kindly invited me to dinner on the Saturday after Thanksgiving. I did not query this offer but graciously accepted. During our friendly chat, she informed me they had taken my advice and adopted a rescue cat.

"The grandchildren adore him!" she exuded joyfully. "They now will sleep over, and they love to have him sleep with them. He follows them all around when they are here and seems to enjoy their company as much as they enjoy his. It's a win-win situation. We are so grateful for your suggestion."

I was reluctant to ask, but I felt I must. "How wonderful for you all, and may I inquire about his colouring and name?"

"He's brown, with a white tummy and paws, so sweet. We waited until the children came so they could name him. They studied him and took their time. After watching an old cat cartoon, they decided on Thomas—short for Thomas O'Malley, an alley cat. Now weren't they clever? The funny thing about this house now, we find, no longer do we have a mysterious catlike lump at our backs in bed." She gave a cheerful laugh. "We have Thomas there instead."

I couldn't resist: "Does Lila still tidy up after you, Edna?"

There was hesitation on the phone before Edna had a memory blackout.

"Tidy up? What are you talking about, Daniel? No one needs ti tidy up after me. See you Saturday next. Keep well! Keep busy! Bye-bye!"

7 GET OFF MY BED

I DRIVE UP TO my cottage in Muskoka as often as I can. It is used in all seasons, and each season brings a never-ending picture book delight. Usually, my relaxation is undisturbed by interference from the somewhere beyond we know little about. Imagine then, my astonishment when early one morning the usual nature sounds of the lake inhabitants failed to be my reliant wake-up call. All was eerily silent. I rolled over in my queen-sized bed, and there she was, lying on the other side facing me!

She was fully clothed in a summer dress. Perhaps fully clothed is an understatement. The dress started just above her full breasts and stopped well above her knees. She was leaning on one elbow, hand under her head, so her dress did little to enclose what seemed to want to escape. The rise of her shapely hip and bent knees showed off her curvaceous form. Her head was on an angle that allowed her long wavy blonde hair to cascade down upon my extra pillow. She was gazing at me with an endearing smile. I sensed she had been waiting until I awakened.

As the grogginess of sleep left my eyes, it dawned on me she was familiar. All of her was too familiar. I did not like this. Was I to go down memory lane to correct juvenile indiscretions?

I waited.

She spoke. "Hi, old friend. Or should I say, old love?" Her voice was more mature than I remembered but just as sexy and suggestive. That was unsettling.

"I know you are surprised to see me like this after all these years. Keep in mind, I'm just as surprised to find myself here. I never came over to your side of the lake very often. Your mother never liked me." She turned away, glided off the bed, and made for the kitchen.

She waited.

I joined her after donning my track pants and tying them tightly. Why I felt I had to defend my mother, I don't know. "Your family were social snobs," I began. "They stayed on the east side in their lakefront summer home and only socialized with us cottage types on Canada Day. It wasn't that Mother disliked you; she never knew you to dislike you. She frowned upon the way you flirted with all the boys."

Stop it, I told myself, *she's got you blathering just like she always could.*

"Put aside the 'woulda, coulda, shoulda' if you will. I'm about to ask for your help." She turned toward me and added with a smile, "If you woulda."

She may have been asking me to set aside old habits, but she was playing on an old secret saying to rope me in. Not fair!

"Tell me your story while I make me my Tims," I told her as I pulled my coffee pot toward me. I wasn't going to admit I was curious how she came to be where she was at a fairly young age.

A cold chill on my neck warned me she was standing behind me much too close, probably mimicking tippy toes and getting ready to whisper sweet nothings in my ear. Still a flirt she was, but not as welcome as she used to be.

"Back off. I want hot coffee, not iced coffee. Go out to the deck. I'll be there in a minute." I imagined her pretty pout but didn't turn to check.

Once outside and settled in my comfy Muskoka chair, holding my favourite cup, I watched her balance on the deck railing, facing me with her back to the lake. I nodded for her to begin her tale.

"Car accident," she stated with no remorse. "Just last year, on my way up here. On the 400 highway near the Innisfil turn-off. Lots of accidents there. Guess it was my fault, as I was in a hurry. You never met my husband, Aadi. He's not from around here. He was very strict and always in control, but I loved him."

She hesitated, waiting for my reaction. I gave her none, so she continued, "His background and religion have led him to believe a woman must remain a virgin until the day she is married. She also is to remain a faithful wife. That part I was fine with, but he thought I should stay in the house and be a happy little housewife, taking care of his every need and wish. The housewife part was no fun. He never wanted to come up here because this was my life before him. He sometimes would ask about the lake and the friends I had up here, but the asking had a negative undertone. If he ever had an inkling of the way we teenagers acted back then, I knew he would become enraged and never forgive me. I would be banished from his life forever. That's why I was in a hurry. I needed to get here before he did."

I had to stop her. "Hold on, Lucy." Her name was not Lucy, but I always called her Lucy. I was Charlie. Same thought, figure it out. "Let's get some order here. You want some help with an earthly problem left undone, I take it. You are aware, are you not, that you must supply a non-monetary payment? A yes or no will suffice."

She nodded in affirmation.

"Let's work backward with this. You won't be here long, judging by the energy you are exerting with your flirting, so let's get down to the brass tacks. What is it you want me to do?"

She put her hands down on the railing and leaned forward. Her shining blonde locks fell in front of her shoulders, thankfully blocking the view of the gaping dress. It was obvious she still knew the power of her loveliness. This was totally unfair for a ghost with past earthly knowledge. She bit her lower lip and cocked her head to the right as if in deep thought. The memory that conjured up was annoying.

I waited.

She straightened up and began. "You do remember don't you, the fun we had here at the lake when all us kids would get together in our boats?"

My turn to nod in affirmation.

"We water skied, motor raced, flipped the blowup rafts. We held bonfire parties and stole our parent's beer, among other things." Her eyes were dreamy with the remembrance, and it was obvious I needed to put a quick end to this or I, too, would have dreamies.

"And you want me to do what?'

She lowered her head and fluttered her eyelashes. "I kept a diary of all my conquests. My goal by the end of our last summer together was to be FWB—you know, friends with benefits—with every boy in our gang, except Dale, of course. He only wanted to be FWB with you." She gave a little giggle as she peeked up. "Guess your mother was right about me."

Mothers usually are, aren't they? But when did adolescent boys ever think they were? Our beach gal Lucy may have kept track of her conquests, but so did we boys. We lined up to see which one of us she would crook her finger at for an evening of sexual delights. Where did she learn that stuff? We were careful to keep the escapades from the steady girlfriends, but not from each other. Did she know that? Did she care? I was alerted to danger signs about this request, so it was best to keep her on track.

"And you want me to do what?'

"My diaries are still at the lake house, in the bunkie. That was my space. You must remember the bunkie, hmmm? Mom and Dad never monitored my comings and goings there." She gave a suggestive smile.

While it is known ghosts and spirits seldom change personalities from their earthly faults, it was still unsettling to be reminded of teenage indiscretions from beyond.

"Aadi and I only had five years together. The lake house was never used during that time. As soon as Dad turned it over to me, Aadi thought we should sell. He wanted the money; I had to agree. He decided he should come up and look around, see if anything could be of use to him.

"Now here is the problem: I have a bookcase full of books in the bunkie. In the evenings by myself, I'd cut out deep holes in the pages of some of them and stuff my wonderful written confessions in there. I told no one. The books look innocent enough; some are mine from when I was a kid. You know, the Carolyn Keene Detective Series, Dr. Seuss's *One Fish, Two Fish*, along with the No. 1 Ladies Detective Agency. The thick hardbacks were great for stuffing.

"Aadi is an avid reader and a lover of books. I knew the first thing he would do when he entered the bunkie would be to go to those books and open them. That's why I was trying to get to the lake ahead of him. I wanted to destroy them all. He has a fierce temper when riled, and that would have riled him, big time. He never made it to the lake. He was driving his car behind me and, of course, stopped at the scene of my demise and never proceeded any further north.

"He has just obtained legal control of the lake house and is planning a much-delayed visit before he sells it. Please, please, dear Charlie," She fluttered those long eyelashes once more. "Motor on over and get those books. They will make a great bonfire. Do this for old times' sake, won't you?"

My Tims special coffee blend was cold by now, and a refill was calling, but she needed to be gone first. "What does it matter now?" I countered. "He can't come back on you no matter what you wrote when you were silly. The guys you knew then most likely have a blank about their summer's discretion or, at best, a pleasant memory about good old what's-her-name."

She wasn't insulted. She never was, as I recall. She smiled that one-upmanship smile glided smoothly off the railing, and came forward to sink into the nearby hammock. The way she curled up, with her legs bent and knees tucked under her chin, was a forerunner to her request.

"It is important that he keeps the fond memories and perfect impression he has of me. I don't want that tarnished because of teenage stupidity. I don't call you Charlie in the diary telling, and there is a lot of telling about you, Danny." She shifted her eyes sideways at me and gave me that knowing smile while she twisted the ends of a loose curl around a finger. "There is a detailed outing of a moonlight zigzag ride across the lake from my place to your cottage. You must remember that night."

Indeed, I did!

"Aadi will fly into a jealous hissy fit if he reads about that night. I did write a good story, you know. He will want affirmation and then exact revenge. He will find you. He will monitor your everyday activities, and when he believes the time is ripe, he will hire a bone breaker or a water boarder. He never does the retaliations himself. He is too far up the food chain for that."

I was now the one with cold chills. *Keep calm and in control*, thought I with a shudder. Bone breaker? Food chain? What country did this Aadi come from?

"And payment?" I squeaked.

"You don't think avoiding broken bones is enough?"

"No, I'm a detective. I can detect and avoid threats."

"You get to read all about my conquests."

"I don't need to indulge in episode 12 of *As the Stomach Churns*."

She thrust her bottom lip forward and kept her head down, those dreamy eyes maintained a half-mast look as she gave it some thought.

A light bulb suddenly dazzled with her final offer. Her energy was running on empty as she raced toward the finish line. "You gave me your grandfather's medal for service from World War II. Do you remember? I got mad at you later and threw it in the lake. I can tell you where I threw it and you can get it."

I remembered this as a take rather than a give. I never knew why she took it or what she did with it, but that was the rationale for no more bunkie visits for me.

I reacted. "You threw it in the lake? You're kidding! Why? What a possessive, jealous bitch you were! The ribbon will be gone and the metal will have deteriorated. We treasured that heirloom."

She flipped her hand dismissively at me. "Oh, cool it, Charlie. It was in that little metal box with the airtight lid, remember? It will be just fine." She ran her finger through her hair, holding it back while she tried for a "you can trust me" look. No more was I falling for trick number nine.

I gave my coffee mug a tight two-handed squeeze and tried for a stern look. "Tell me where and how."

"Blueberry Island. About six metres out from the rock point, where we used to skinny dip. She gave her skinny dipping giggle. "That is the where; the how is up to you. The bunkie key is still in the usual hidey-hole. You must remember where that is." And she was gone like a whisper in the wind.

The loons, frogs, and cicadas brought back the wonderous lake sounds.

I could not remember if she told me when her Aadi was coming up, but it behooved me to take a nonchalant trip over to the moneyed side of the lake as soon as possible. I chose to take my aluminum fishing boat, with its small motor, as the fish finder was still attached to the side. My reasoning was I could take a detour over to the rock point on the way back and take a precursory gaze down six metres out on the off chance of catching a glimpse of Great Grandpa's little metal box containing his African Star medal.

One step at a time in orderly measure was needed. Roadblocks should be dealt with as they arise, so my detecting skills afford me. Lay claim to the bunkie key from the hidey-hole with the hope no other of her past conquests had been there and gained knowledge of her written pleasures before me.

A slow ride across the lake works wonders as a form of therapy. All senses work as one. As the head is held high, the fresh breezes blow through thinning hair, massaging the scalp and one can smell nature's pureness. The dancing ripples slap against the side of the vessel in a rhythmic summer song.

Diamonds sparkle as far as one can see across the stretch of changing blues. They are forever on the move. Rimmed all around the edges are the fifty shades of green bestowed upon the land. The contour of the horizon shapes the growth as it is outlined against the upper blueness holding an array of white puffiness.

Too soon, the lake house came into view. It had been a few years since I had made my way over to this side of the lake. I heard the echo of teenage times as I steered out into the middle of the lake to circle the boat tightly, bow rising, without reversing—the macho way of young lads. I turned and approached the dock on the far side. I cut the purr of the motor and glided to the dock, placing the loop of the boat rope over the top rung of the ladder. This ritual was not forgotten. It was on automatic pilot after all these years.

The boat rocked gently as it settled, and the slap of the small waves against the wooden dock still rated as one of my favourite sounds. The smell of water on wood makes one bow one's head, close eyes, and thank the God of Nature. No prayer in any cathedral can be equal in its pureness.

I gave my humble thanks, climbed the three rungs onto the dock and gazed at the lake house. I had never been inside. The bunkie was as far as I had ever been. It was still there, to the right and back further on the property than the house itself. Time had been kind to it. It stood on stilts a metre off the ground, giving an area to store outside play toys. The sides were shingled brown and the roof red. Three wide steps led up to the wrap-around deck sans railings. There were only two posts situated at a distance to comfortably tie a hammock that would hold two. Thanks for the memory, Lucy!

The dock I stood on was windswept, but the water on each side held small twigs and a few years' collections of flora.

Some boards would need to be replaced soon, as the rot of ages was claiming their rightful hold. The crunch of leaves and small branches made delightful sounds as I worked my way up and to the right of the house. I stood in front of the bunkie.

Meeting her in the bunkie was the end of the treasure map she laid out. Around the bend of the property was an inlet covered with brush known only to the boys. One did not tie up at the front dock at the close of the day. Once securing a small craft at the inlet, one stealthily proceeded over the mossy bed and around the monstrous boulder that blocked the view from the house to the bunkie. Snuggled behind the boulder, one would find two rocks standing knee-high to the chosen boy. A division between them held a flat dinner-plate-sized rock. Upon lifting it, one then spied the hidey-hole. Within the hidey-hole, all one could see was the round green lid of a plastic peanut butter jar. Inside the jar tied with many ribbons that seemed to multiply throughout the summer. was the key to an upcoming adventure. This made for exciting foreplay as one continued through the dark and finally, with the turn of the key, into the bunkie and Lucy.

No need to make the journey from the inlet this time. I straight-lined directly to the two knee-high rocks. The dinner plate was still in its place, surrounded by shoots of tender maple saplings attempting to grow from teenage size to adults. Balancing with one hand on a rock, I grasped the plate and raised one end out of its bed. I was met with a village of active ground bugs, slugs, and worms. Peeking through their dung was the green plastic lid of the infamous peanut butter jar.

The village inhabitants scattered as best they could due to my raid, and I whisked away the remaining few with the leftover debris. Using my fingers and thumb around the edge of the lid, I loosened the jar with a rocking motion and it rose upward with little resistance. The lid itself needed to be coaxed open. It seemed too tired to cooperate after lying dormant for so long. Peering inside, I spied the key with many ribbons tied through the ring at the head. No longer were they shouting out their mystery of colours, but with their age, they all had faded to a sad colourless nothingness. I pulled the mess out carefully, as deterioration was added to the mix.

I took the time to replace the jar and stone plate. Why? I do not know. In reverence to bygone days or to aid in rebuilding the village, perhaps?

I straightened, flicked the forest collection off my knees, and was bunkie bound.

The key remembered its purpose without hesitation, and once I stood inside, it was as if time rewound uncomfortably. All was the same, except the bedding, mattress, and curtains had been removed. It seemed sensible that all cloth materials should be taken out at the end of each summer season to avoid the intrusion of the forest's unwanted guests.

The one-room bunkie was smaller than I remembered. It measured no more than six or seven metres. It held a bunk bed, mirrored dresser, and bookcase. Girlish posters and knick-knacks were taking up space wherever they could. The one window gave a perfect view of the lake. All was musty, airless, and spider webby.

Four steps took me to the bookcase. Lucy had amassed an interesting collection. It covered thick, thin, hardcover, softcover, magazines, newspapers, and most genres you could think of. A complicated girl, she was. Most of the five shelves were tightly packed, leaving little room for even one more addition. I placed a forefinger on top of the spine of a thick hardcover and pulled it forward. Dust, spiders, and mouse droppings poured forth. I let go and it fell back in place.

I was contemplating my next move when I heard the slam of a car door followed by the muffled sounds of male voices. I froze. I waited.

Two men came into view. The window faced southwest, so this time of day rendered me only silhouettes. They were not big men, nor did they look threatening. By the sing-song sway of their vocalization, I clued into the fact they were speaking ESL (English as a second language). I thought immediately of Lucy's husband.

They walked slowly by the bunkie as they surveyed the area. It was obvious they were in new territory. One spied my boat and pointed it out to the other. They walked over to and along the length of the dock, checked out my vessel, and visually searched back toward the house, assuming there must be a body to go along with the boat. I needed to make my presence known. Stick to the truth as much as possible. Try to avoid broken bones or waterboarding.

I stepped outside through the open doorway and stood on the deck. "Well, hello there! Can I help you?" I hoped I sounded more confident than I felt as I waited to see what attitude I would get in response.

They both looked my way in surprise. One raised his hand in salutation, and they both commenced walking toward me.

I stepped down to the ground and waited once more.

As they came into view, without the sun as background, it was plain they were of East Indian descent.

The one who hadn't waved, spoke. "Hello!" He sported a flashing white smile. " I'm Aadi Singh; this is my brother, Royh, and you are?"

"Just one of the cottagers on the lake." I shrugged my shoulders, showing them I was of no importance. "Once in a while as we motor by, we stop in and check to make sure everything is okay. No fallen trees causing damage, no animals nesting, no broken windows." My voice cracked on the word broken. "And you are here because?" I carried on feigning ignorance.

"My wife's family owned this place. They have all passed on. Shirley was my wife. Surely, you knew Shirley?" He looked at me as if to acquire acknowledgement he had made good with an English play on words.

Brother Royh spoke up for the first time. With a large smile and clapping his hands, he asked, "You fish? You have a fish finder in your fishing boat, but no fishing poles. How come that is? We love to fish very much too."

Although Royh was the age and size of an adult, it was obvious he had a disability.

Aadi pulled his brother's hands down and held them. He addressed me once more. "Can you show me around? I'm not sure what to do here. I know Shirley loved this place, but for some reason, she never wanted me to come up. She said that life was gone, and her life started again with me. That made me very curious."

I didn't detect violence in these men, but one never knows, does one? He had just stated a contradiction. I needed to get rid of the diaries and bid them ado.

"I don't have a key to the house, but you must have one if you are now the owner. I can show you the property lines if you wish. Come out to the back. You can follow the tree line up over that hill."

My strategy was to grab the books and vacate while they walked over the rise. Not so, however, as Aadi noticed the bunkie's open door.

"You were in there when we arrived. Why was that?" he asked as he made for the bunkie.

"Just checking on tiny varmints that like tiny houses."

"Find any?"

"Nope!"

Aadi, with brother Royh right behind, was now entering the bunkie. I knew from experience three would be one too many to fit inside, so I shaded my eyes and watched Aadi through the filthy, cobwebbed window. As Shirley/Lucy predicted, he made right for the bookcase, bent over, hands on knees, and checked out the titles on the spines in much the same manner I had minutes before.

And then he did it. He reached out and pulled the thickest hardcover out of its home and held it by his fingers while he shook and blew off as much of the accumulated debris as possible. I held my breath as I watched him open the front cover. We had different expectations, and neither was fulfilled.

There was a whirl of wind that brought forth a snowfall of tiny pieces of paper litter. Kudos to Aadi's bravery, he did not drop the book but merely jolted in surprise, causing another shower of minuscule garbage to float through the air and land upon the floorboards. He looked up, turned in disgust, and thrust the book toward Royh for a look. They both came out of the bunkie, Aadi still holding the book. He held it out for my inspection. Most pages had been cut away leaving a neat well, approximately three centimetres deep. Cautiously peeking in, I spied the mummified remains of five newborn mice. I was relieved.

"Well, that's nature," said I, the wise one.

Royh made for the dock and my boat once more. Aadi closed the cover of the book with a snap, causing more litter to fly. "I suppose," he ventured, "every book will be contaminated this way?"

"I suppose." I was quick to agree. "There's a fire pit down near the shoreline. Best to take it all down there and burn it."

"I want to look around and see what I got here. I do have a key for the house and the boathouse. Tomorrow, I will just burn down that tiny house. Save carrying all those filthy books and papers out. The building looks like it is ready to fall anyway."

Was this guy for real, or did he just like big bonfires?

"Can't happen," I informed him. "You would have the fire marshal, truck, and police for company just as soon as the smoke cleared the treetops. You would be handed major fire fines."

"Will you take me fishing?" Royh's voice directly behind me caused me to jump, and it wasn't for joy. How did he sneak up so quickly and quietly?

Time for a defensive attitude to test the waters. "I'll leave you to it then. Nice to have met you. Have a good day." After delivering these platitudes and waving one hand over my head, I headed to my escape launch. I was not in my detecting mode—no, not one bit.

"Hold up!" Aadi called out as he hurried after me with Royh on his heels. "Do you know someone who lost his family's war medal?"

That caused me to hold up, a suspiciously confusing hold-up.

I turned to face the two of them and waited.

"Come back," he continued. "If you could please give me some of your time, I would like to have a quick look around and then could we talk for a few minutes? There are questions I would like to ask someone who knew my wife when she spent her summers up here."

"And we could go fishing," Royh chimed in hopefully, wearing a bright smile on his brown face. What was with this guy? Was he as waterproof as he appeared, or was this an act heading toward sinister deeds?

Staying for a Lucy chat was not something I wanted to do, but he had dangled the line of the war medal as an offer I couldn't refuse.

"Go wander about" was the best I could come up with. "I'll bring those books and papers down to the fire pit and burn them." He gave a shrug that indicated "whatever."

I headed to my boat to retrieve my recycle blue box and butane lighter. Royh was on my heels, hoping, I suppose for a fishing expedition. I handed him the blue box to carry up to the bunkie, and he quite willingly helped me load it with the aforesaid materials. He followed directions eagerly, and I was convinced this fellow could never be a bone breaker.

I stirred the fire around the edges of the pit, keeping the flames low. I had no tantalizing desire to open the books for a peek at her scribbling. Embers glowed and small blackened bits were fluttering dizzily upwards. *Goodbye, yellow brick road*, I mused.

Royh and I went down to the shoreline and washed our hands and faces as best we could. We sat on the dock, and Royh's small talk confirmed he was Aadi's younger brother and a ward in his care.

It was not long before we heard the sound of Aadi's leather-soled city shoes clumping on the wooden deck, then felt him hunkering down in place beside us.

"Tell me now,' he began without fanfare, "would you know anyone that lost a family's African Star medal?"

Sometimes, life takes us around bends and corners we never see coming, or we are not given a foothold or mainstay to relate to a situation. Never could I have foreseen that I would be sitting on this particular lake house dock, telling the family story of my great-grandfather, a proud Canadian soldier fighting with the British Desert Rats, to a couple of East Indians I had met just a short while ago under peculiar circumstances. Yet, there I was, with their undivided attention.

My great-grandfather served under General Harding in the North African campaign against General Rommel, the Desert Fox in World War II. Aadi asked for a description of the medal, and I had to rack my memory cells. I could only remember Commonwealth medals differed by the colours on the ribbons. The yellow copper medal was the same; I did remember the box it was in. I fluffed over the telling of how I had lost said article. I was not sure why I was taking such pains to explain this to Aadi, but I knew Lucy was always capable of inventing a whole new truth to suit any situation. Did Aadi know something about Gramps's medal that I didn't?

I sensed the day was waning, as the view of the lake showed a golden pathway across its length. The sun was quickly bidding its farewell.

I bounced back on my rear, bent my knees, and stood. "I need to go, guys. It'll be dark soon."

They both turned around and stood as well. Aadi faced me.

"I have your medal," he said. "You see, my great-grandfather was in that campaign too. India was part of the Commonwealth, just like Canada and Australia. The medals are the same, as you know, but the colours of the ribbons differ. My father was heartbroken that somewhere over the years, our family medal was lost. He lamented and told a heroic story about his grandfather and how he earned his medal.

Shirley and I had a conversation about this," he continued. "She had a habit of showing up with unique articles. I never questioned her about them. One day, she presented my father with this medal, saying she found it in an antique shop. The ribbon and back marks identified it as a Canadian African Star. My father never noticed the difference and was grateful to have it. I never questioned how she came to have it, but something told me it was not from an antique shop.

"Next weekend, we'll come back up and I'll bring it with me. Could you come over, say on Saturday? Perhaps around noon?"

I was rendered speechless. I nodded my head and climbed down the three-rung ladder and into my boat. As I untied and drifted out to start the motor, I heard Royh shout, "Can we go fishing?" That lad had a one-track mind.

"Your name!" Aadi shouted. "You never told me your name!"

"Oh! Just call me Charlie!"

While preparing for my Saturday motor over to the lake house, I decided to take along enough fishing gear for three people. Royh's request was echoing in my ear. That city boy had never experienced fishing in a pristine Muskoka lake. Sometimes, I can reach out.

As I approached the dock at the agreed upon time, it was obvious the two brothers had been there long enough to make themselves at home. Doors and windows were open, lawn furniture was in place, and there they sat soaking up the high-noon sun.

Royh waved wildly when he recognized my boat. He jumped up and ran to the end of the dock and stood there until I was landlocked.

"You have fishing poles this time. You will take me fishing?" The big smile and eager tone could not be refused. I was afraid if I did, he would burst out in tears.

"Sure, for a little while, in a little while." I was noncommittal as I marched down the dock toward Aadi, who had not moved out of his chair but just waited.

I sat in the chair vacated by Royh and waited too. Aadi was sipping on a cool one and made no move to offer me one. He would have to learn cottage etiquette if he was thinking of becoming a Muskoka weekender.

"I brought the medal," he finally said. "It's in the house. Come with me. I'll get it."

"I'll wait here if it's all the same to you." I had no desire to enter the house.

Aadi rose, taking his drink with him. He turned and headed for the house. I looked out over the lake, and a ripple of "all is right with the world" flowed through my being. The lake was still. Royh sat cross-legged on the dock, quietly waiting and guarding the boat and fishing gear.

"Here it is, still in the box." The spell was shattered. Aadi handed me the small tin box that had housed the medal for over seventy-five years.

I held the box reverently and smoothed the top with both thumbs, then slowly opened the lid. It came off easier than I had anticipated. It had been viewed I suppose by Aadi and others recently. There, it lay. I had not seen it in quite some time, but the colours had not faded, nor had the ribbons become worn. The six-pointed star shone just as proudly as I expected it did the day it was pinned upon my great's chest.

"Thank you, Aadi." I put the lid back on, stood and reached to shake his hand. "It means a lot to me to have it back." He nodded his head just once. I looked out at the dock and the still figure of Royh. "I have time to take him fishing. Will you come?"

"That's very kind of you, but no, go ahead. I need to look around some more and see what has to be done. I have decided to sell. Too many memories here that are not mine." With that, he headed back up to the house. I rose and strode back to the boat and a wide-eyed, smiling Royh.

Sometimes, when you head into a situation you don't expect to enjoy, you find, instead, you get double the pleasure. Royh was enthused about the whole venture, and it was more catching than the measles. He made me aware of incidents I had taken for granted for years.

"*What makes a frog hop one way when he could hop another?*" "*Why are some trees greener than others?*" "*The same birds have different calls.*" "*Why do big fish eat little fish?*" Why indeed! Through the limited senses of Aadi's brother, I did not have the answers, but he did not let up on the questions. He was very inquisitive and draining. The good Lord managed to let him catch a fish to top off his experience. His excitement was contagious.

While this was quite an unusual happening for me, I was ready to bring the day to a close. After giving Aadi some asked for advice on real estate, I bid them both a fond farewell and motored back over to my comfortable side of the lake.

Teenage Lucy's provocative writings were now gone. All the secrets she stored inside the book covers became mouse homes and then rose from the ashes as little blackened bits of nothingness. I had my family medal back in an unexpected way. I was left a little resentful at Lucy's fabrications. It should not have bothered me she was still true to her human form. She could spin a tale every which way suited her purpose and never blink an eye if caught in a web of her own making. She would just laugh it off with a flip of her hair.

It was another month before I went to my cottage once more, and a nostalgic turn by the lake house showed me a for sale sign emblazoned with a large red "SOLD" banner across it. It hadn't taken Aadi long to make good on his decision. I was happy for him and felt self-satisfied for giving Royh the gift of Muskoka. We all need to reach around and pat ourselves on the back once in a while if we can reach that far.

That evening, as I lounged comfortably, Muskoka ale in hand, watching a Blue Jays' game, I spied a slight movement out of the corner of my eye coming from my bedroom. I had left the door ajar, and as I turned my head and shoulders in that direction for a better look, I was met with a full-body view of Lucy. Once again, she was lying on her side, still wearing the flimsy dress, holding her head up with her hand on a bent elbow. She was gazing out the open door with a dreamy, satisfied smile on her lovely face.

"Aw, come on, Lucy." I put my beer down but stayed right where I was. "We're done here. Your tall tales about what kind of man your husband was and what you did with the medal were all lies. It doesn't matter now anyway. Your diaries, probably exaggeration personified, are gone, never to be read, but did, if I might add, give comfort to a mouse birthing. I have my medal back; found your husband and his brother to be much nicer than what you deserved. Now, get off my bed, go back, and find some unsuspecting ghostly man to play your silly games." I picked up my beer after delivering my speech and turned away from her.

Lucy got off my bed and slunk out the half-open doorway with the ease of no door in the way. She sashayed her way across my den, turned her back to the view, leaned against the sliding glass door, and, pouting that sexy pout, delivered her Lucy reasoning.

"Let me tell you now about my Aadi. He is an exceptional man. He treated me with all the care and love any wife could ask for. He looks after his disabled stepbrother and had looked after his long-term-care parents. His father thought he was still in their small village in India and needed desperately to go and search for their belongings that were swept away during a monsoon. The one item that was sorely lost was his grandfather's African Cross medal. Well, you see, Charlie, I did still have yours. Yes, I took it. Just a play of words, don't you think? I didn't know there was a difference, and Aadi's father didn't notice. He became quite peaceful as he held that tiny tin box so tenderly. He passed away not long ago.

"Royh is Aadi's father's son from his second marriage in India, but Aadi has always loved and cared for him. He had hired an influential and expensive lawyer to get Royh into Canada. When Royh arrived, he was holding a fishing magazine. All he could talk about was going fishing in a boat. Aadi is not comfortable in a boat, especially small ones. Need I go on about the pleasure you gave to Royh? I know you enjoyed the outing too.

"Aadi worked very hard building up his import/export business to meet his responsibilities. I wanted to sell the lake house so he would have some finances to kick-start his dreams, but he was adamant he was not going to take my inheritance.

"I was on my way up not only to get rid of my diaries but to put the lake house on the market before he could talk me out of it."

I could see she was fading after all this exertion but knew she needed to finish her dramatic reasons why. I waited. I refused to look at her but did not interrupt.

"If I told you this boring little story, what fun would that have been? I may have been a teenage problem, but I never was a bore, was I? Now come on, my Charlie, wasn't it fun to find the hidey-hole once more and check out the bunkie? You shoulda, coulda, but never woulda. Just thank me for the memory, and I will thank you for helping my two men."

She smiled her smile, blew a kiss, and didn't wait for a response. But then, she never did.

8 DISAPPEARING GOLF BALLS

QUITE OFTEN THE GIVER of assignments at CODA sends me to places that take me out of the city. Welcome assignments they are too, as they give me a chance to dig into the dusty corners of our expansive province. Such it was when I was prepped on an assignment to King Township, near Lloydtown. *Oh, happy day*, thought I. I was hoping that unique antique and collectible store was still there. So many of them had closed lately. I decided I would leave early so I could meander through towns and villages along the way.

But those plans quickly became mashed potatoes when I spied the Trails Golf Club as the designated destination! A golf club hidden away so well in the countryside that no one had heard of it?

The giver of assignments soon set me straight. He handed me a pamphlet outlining the history of the Carrying Place Trail. It showed me interesting places by the name of Schomberg, Kettleby, and Pottageville, to name a few.

"The Trails Golf Club is hard by this historic trail," he informed me. "The club is very selective in its membership, hence the reason why it is known only to those who take the game seriously.

"It appears," he continued, "they have a case of disappearing golf balls. They need a golfing detective to detect the thievery. This private club has its golden reputation at stake."

"Disappearing?" asked I. "Don't you mean lost?" All my query got me was a disappearing frown as the giver of assignments disappeared.

I knew if this case needed a detective wise to the ways of obsessed golfers rich enough to be members of a club like this, I shouldn't be that sleuth. I am a fair-weather golfer with no handicap attached.

I gave a practiced grumble and groan and was, therefore, dangled an offer I couldn't refuse: CODA was prepared to pony up for two weeks of practice on the links, after which I would be deemed a CODA professional golfer. No lessons included, just some practice time.

I picked the mothballs out of my golf bag, afraid of what I might find at the bottom. Little creatures do make their way into the best of garages, don't they? I shined up my old golf shoes, checked out my favourite clubs, and shined them up too. I then took myself down to Golf Town. 'Twas there I treated myself to a new glove and a box of Callaway golf balls. I told them not to disappear. I headed down to the Docks a few times and had some serious misunderstandings at the driving range and the putting green. I must admit it did feel good to be out there and attempt to get back into the swing of things—pun intended.

The next step was to convince three buddies to give up a day for the sake of my upcoming assignment. Better golfers than I, they groaned with green eyes when I let it slip where I was heading. I let them bribe me into buying the beers on the nineteenth if they would make up a foursome for me at one of Aurora's public courses.

I encouraged them to be critical of my game, and any useful pointers would be welcome. I got the usual comments: "Do you know where the fairway is?" "You're a little short there, Alice." "You swing like a girl." "You can use the front tees if you want."

The following week I cruised up to my cottage and joined a couple of local friends at the Bracebridge public golf course. They were more polite: "Nice shot." "You should be able to get out of the rough from there." "Everyone lands that sand trap once in a while. Do you want a mulligan?"

Ready or not, it was soon time to head to the Trails. I purposely left my clubs at home just in case I was asked if I wanted to play a round. I would be all business in my detecting.

Going north out of Toronto is a drive I always appreciate. I chose to veer over to the King Sideroad and drive up on back roads—a slower drive but not too crowded early in the morning. This route used to be dotted with family farms, but more and more, it is becoming plastered with oversized houses in overpriced lots.

Before long, I spied the impressive sign and distinctive logo pointing the way forth to the golf course and clubhouse. The well-manicured approach showed off gardens of wildflowers interspersed with a variety of hostas and pine growths. Upon entering the grounds, one's eye could view the rising landscape of some of the fairways. Early morning enthusiasts could be spied wielding their weapons in a knowing macho manner. The dew was still on the fairway, but the grounds crew was making good headway vacuuming the greens.

I slowed, then braked my SUV and lowered the window to take in the wonderous scene and turn up nature's audio. The multi sounds of the birds from robins to crows sang in harmony with the occasional cheekiness of the chipmunks and the scolding of the squirrels. I fancied the holes near the water, as there, nature would add the drumroll of the bullfrogs and the clash of the cranes. I gave myself a little time to be attentive to the symphony. Sometimes, the joy of roaming a golf course allows one to be appreciative of this gift.

My solitude and commune did not last long. It was abruptly interrupted by a sharp voice reprimanding me.

"About time you got here. What took you so long? Let's go!"

He was standing just off the freshly painted curb, looking very sporty and fit. I ventured a guess he was in his late thirties. He was wearing not only the club's collared shirt with an embroidered logo, but also the confidence that goes along with being a well-respected member of the club. Money speaks. His taper-fitted golf slacks showed off his well-developed muscular legs right down to his spike-less FootJoys. He had his arms crossed with his hands tucked under his armpits—all the better to view his biceps.

His full head of dark hair was trimmed and moulded to perfection, aside from a tiny loose strand placed exactly at an angle on his forehead. It pointed to the full dark eyebrows formed over his dazzling blue eyes. He would have been handsome, if not for the scowl he was directing my way.

I initially thought he was from the club house sent on the mission of identifying my vehicle, but as he glided effortlessly toward my open window and placed his arms on the door, the waft of frigid air he brought along told a different story.

I waited. He did not.

"I've got an unfinished game to finish. It's been over a year. I need your physical presence to let me do that. Details won't matter much; I'll be in control. You just relax and go along for the ride. You're a golfer? You'll enjoy the game."

Slow it down. Lower the temperature. Take a breath. I did not need to ask if he was a ghost or a spirit, as only spirits are so impolite and seek control. It seemed he was doomed to stay on course in more ways than one. My manners teed off.

"Back up! You're not my first round. I know the ground rules better than you do. If you want my help, it has to be given not taken. So far, I can see right through your attitude."

He missed my very clever pun, as he came back with, "I'll ride along with you and explain the deal."

"Like hell, you will!" I spat. He jolted, and I smelled a slight hellfire singe. "If you have been waiting over a year, you can damn well wait a little longer. I need to get to the clubhouse and look after some business. Meanwhile, you can think about how long and involved this help is going to be, and based on those two factors, you better come up with a substantial payment."

He silently backed away from my window while daggers shot forth from his dark baby blues. If this was a violent demise, he would soon be disqualified. As I slowly began moving forward, a lightbulb came on.

I braked and looked back. "By the way, have you anything to do with disappearing golf balls?"

He faded off into a mist, leaving an echo of a satisfied "gottcha" chuckle.

The golf manager and the pro were quite amiable when the shopkeeper announced my arrival. They escorted me out to the granite patio. The Muskoka lawn chairs were painted in hues of nature's softest shades. The wide arms gave room for the papers and pamphlets they provided containing an extensive outline of each hole and all pertinent information I might need. All was well, they explained without further ado—except for the weird phenomenon around the green on the fifteenth fairway.

"Explain," I asked. I crossed my legs, settled back with a club monogrammed pen in hand, scribbled "15th" on the monogrammed club paper, and waited.

They were silent while the server placed monogrammed coffee mugs on the small tables between us. Manager then leaned forward and commenced his tale. It appeared he would be the one to tell, with a backup correction if needed from Pro.

It proved to be a little difficult to give him my full attention, as at the mention of the fifteenth fairway, the roadside spirit suddenly hovered near my left side. He looked down at my hand in fury.

"You're left-handed! How was I to know! This is ridiculous! This won't work. I've waited for nothing. You're worthless! *Arrgghh!*"

He jerked his head back and threw his arms up in anger. I sensed he was about to send the pen, paper, and maybe the coffee mugs flying across the patio. Looking at Manager, I could see his mouth moving, but his voice was dialled to a decibel I couldn't hear. I needed control.

I stood up, with an "Excuse me, it's been a long trip; I need a pit stop."

He held the mouth movement, looked insulted, and pointed the way.

Once out of sight and sound, I was able to lower the temp and close over the weak spot in my aura. *Deal with that later,* I told myself.

Retracing my steps and offering a sincere apology, I concentrated on the tale to be told.

"Some weird stuff is going on at the fifteenth," Manager continued. Pro nodded his agreement and encouragement as they looked at each other. I sensed they were serious men afraid I would scoff and think them foolish. Oh, if they only knew!

He continued, "It's a par fifty-four hundred yards, give or take. Not the longest one, but can be tricky. You tee off over water, keeping right. Now if you get up near the green and have a short chip, everything is fine."

He stopped, reached for his coffee, and took a sip before continuing. "The problem is . . ." He set his mug back down and looked me defiantly in the eye. "You're a golfer, right?"

He didn't ask for a handicap or to define a golfer, so I shook my head in affirmation.

"If one of our members hits a long fairway shot and manages to get up on the green or even into one of the bunkers, he finds when he gets there, his ball is gone. Just gone! He and his group have seen it land and it looks really good, you know? They're anxious to check it out, but when they approach, it's simply not there." He stopped, still staring me down, and waited, daring my reaction.

He didn't have an inkling of my background sources, so how in control and superior, I felt, if even for a small amount of time. We all get our jollies somehow.

Quietly and oh so wisely of me, I asked, "What causes have you eliminated?"

He settled back and threw a hitchhiker's thumb at Pro and wearily said, "Jim?"

Jim Pro then became the spokesperson. "Kids, we thought, running up and taking off, but we would have seen them. A dog playing catch and escaping into the bush area, but again, we would have seen. A drainage ditch or water hole? A flying bird looking for a meal? None of these panned out. If the ball landed in one of the bunkers, we could see the roll line and then nothing where the line stopped. We would search the grass and ground all around the edges. No ball! Nothing! We have even posted a marshal at that green during tournaments, and would you believe, no one at that time managed a long shot!

"We have had some very upset members and guests this year. It seems they would be playing an exceptional game, and then this would happen. It would blow them right out of the standings. We can't afford to lose members or our reputation because of a quirky happening."

He looked at me with skepticism. "To tell you the truth, Detective, we have no idea what you can do about this, but your agency was suggested and you're our last hope, so why not?"

I didn't need his insult and injury plowing down on my moment of superiority and control, but balloons were meant to be burst and he had a point.

I cleared my throat for effect as I leaned forward. To mix my sports, the ball was now in my court. "I'll go out and have a good look around if you don't mind. Can I take a cart?"

"Of course. Either Jim or I will go with you. Give you a guided tour, if you will."

That, I figured, I would get—but not from either of them. I had to be plausible.

"I'd prefer to drive the back nine alone, staying on the cart path, checking out imaginary shots, until I settle in on the fifteenth. Fresh eyes and all that. I will surely have questions and need your input when we drive out together later."

The men gave each other brief eye contact and affirmative head nods. "That's reasonable," Manager conceded, "but there's another thing we should let you know about the fifteenth fairway."

Here it comes: a big piece of the puzzle.

"Last year, we lost one of our members on that hole."

"Lost? You mean as in disappeared like the golf balls?" I held my left hand up near my ear and clicked my finger and thumb for effect.

"No, no." They both held their mouth in a manner that suggested they were trying not to laugh. Manager continued, "You should never speak ill of the dead, lest the devil catches you 'round the corner. Actually, I think he did catch Troy Black." Again, they both looked at each other, trying for sombre that didn't work.

I waited.

"Troy was a good golfer, but he thought he was terrific. He was taking part in an in-house tournament, having a terrific game, and true to form, he was replaying each hole after each play, letting his team know how he had accomplished each terrific shot and what they were doing wrong with their game. None of the other members ever wanted to play with him and weren't too happy when it was their turn to team up with him. They referred to him as Troy Terrific, and he thought it was a compliment."

I waited.

Jim Pro took over the narration. "He was racking up the birdies and pars as if the devil himself had a hand in it. He was extremely excited and was mentally in the clubhouse, seeing his name at the top of the scoreboard and accepting trophies for low and best everything. He had hit a long shot to the front of the green and seemed to be staggering forth oddly. The others thought at first he was just being Troy putting on one of his performances. They reported, he suddenly stopped, leaned on his chipping wedge, grabbed at his chest, gasped, and collapsed."

Jim stopped and looked at me for my reaction. I gave the same as I received. Stonewall. He continued, "By the time they called us and 9-1-1 and a paramedic helicopter had landed on the fairway, it was obvious Troy Terrific Black would never get to finish the terrific game he was having."

Don't count your golf balls before they disappear, thought I, once more being ever so clever. *Troy Terrific is on the move.*

"Well, that's about it," Jim Pro finalized as they both got to their feet. "I'll have one of the boys bring a cart around flying a marshal flag. No one will question you. Be careful not to interfere with anyone's game. We have some earlies out there this morning."

━━━

A beautiful cart, it was indeed. Washed and polished to a twinkle. There was bottled water to drink, a towel and water to clean clubs, sand to fill divots, and even three complimentary golf balls sporting the club logo. It had backup and brake lights and a vocalized GPS that gave a play-by-play of each hole as you approached. Beeps and bells warned of impending danger if you strayed off the designated areas of travel. It was a golf cart driver's heavenly dream. I expected this heavenly dream would soon be brought down to Earth by the appearance of Troy Terrific Black.

I ignored the front nine and deked around behind the clubhouse to start my drive from the tenth tee box. The course was well manicured, with rolling hills, incidental dips, and side issues designed to give a challenge to serious players. It was well above the ability of a weekend warrior like me. I had only the length of the tenth fairway to appreciate the beauty when Troy Terrific made his debut beside me in the cart.

He wasted no time. "A par four and I birdied it. It was a terrific drive; used my three wood. Carried it straight and long. My nine iron placed it on the green right where I knew how to roll with the bend of the grass. Once you know a course, it's yours to command."

He was sitting up straight, holding the hand grasp near the top of the roof. His gaze told me he considered himself master of all he surveyed.

He then turned to face me, showing disgust on his face and defeat in his body. "You're left-handed," he accused me once more. "I saw you writing with your left hand. The effort to control you playing right-handed will wear me out too quickly, and there is no way I can swing backward like you. You're useless."

With that, he slumped back and pouted. *Live with it,* I thought. There was no way I was going to enlighten him and confess my golf and baseball games were conducted in a right-handed style. That was probably why I didn't excel. Let him pout.

The magnificent cart was telling me the tenth green was on my left and the next turn would be to the right, staying on the path through the pine trees.

"Mute that! Button on the bottom. Just listen to me!"

He was a difficult being even after his demise. I hit the button on the bottom and slowed the cart to a crawl as I tried to maintain control. Without it, this would be a no-go.

"Troy Terrific, what an egocentric ass you were and still are. Didn't it bother you that no one liked you or wanted to partner with you?"

"Ha!" he sneered, turning to look out the side of the cart. "That's the way people act when they are jealous of another man's accomplishments. They gang together to discredit people like me. You just have to show your superiority and overcome the lessers."

He had not looked back at me. No eye contact gives one many clues. I stopped the cart and waited.

He finally turned and hedged some more. "Well, drive on. What are you waiting for? We need to get to the fifteenth so I can show you what happened. By the way, where are your clubs? What kind of clubs do you use?"

"I didn't bring my clubs. No intention of playing today. I don't play well. My clubs are just a mixture of many." Why did I even bother to answer?

He gave a pained expression. "It doesn't matter. You'll need to use mine. Take them with you and practise golfing the right way: right-handed. They're still at the clubhouse, in my locker."

He chuckled meanly. "No one knows the combination of my lock. They're thinking of sawing it off, but that is destroying private property, so they have to wait until my dues expire. I'll give you the code. Figure it out."

It was time to talk turkey. "I don't like you any more than the club members did. I am not inclined to take on an assignment with you, but I'll give you from now until we arrive at the fifteenth to explain what you have in mind and what your payment would be. Start now. You haven't much time." With that, I began a smooth right turn through the pines.

"I think you should know how I played each hole up to the fourteenth."

"No."

"You need to get the flavour of how I was anticipating each shot before I swung."

"No."

"Have you had a chance to check out my unfinished scorecard?"

"No, and we are approaching the twelfth, so you have three more holes to answer my two questions before I'm out of here."

His need outweighed his vanity at this point, as he suddenly burst forth in a static-like voice. "I need to finish this game. I was so close. Just four more holes. I would have won it all. I would have gained all the respect I deserved. They would have had to say 'Troy Terrific' in a whole different way. I want to use you to finish my game unless you know someone who would be better than you. I have built up and know how to use my energy to do that. We will start on the first and play it just as I had. I'll guide you through each shot. When we get to the fifteenth, the work begins. I'll adjust you the way I want. You gotta cooperate, as by then, I will be starting to weaken. You'd better not blow this. Your payment will be a hole-in-one. You can't deny that every golfer, even duffers like you, want bragging rights for that."

"You're wrong," I corrected him much too quickly. "I've never even thought about a hole-in-one. That wouldn't be sufficient payment for having to put up with you engineering my physical being for four hours. The thought makes me want to puke."

"I'll throw in my full set of TaylorMades."

Our negotiation was interrupted when I spied, motoring toward me, a real course marshal.

"Oh boy, here comes Sergeant Major Larry," Troy spat out sarcastically. "I gotta go. Someone just hit a long shot on the fifteenth."

———

Larry, contrary to the detrimental term applied by Troy Terrific, was quite cordial. He knew who I was and why I was there but wondered why I had turned off the GPS. He asked politely if I would wait just a while until the foursome on the thirteenth finished on the green before I proceeded forward. Of course, it wasn't a problem to oblige.

While I sat in the luxurious cart, sipping Pure Life spring water, my mind did some golf wandering. Deep down, perhaps I really did covet the thrill of claiming a hole-in-one. Logically speaking, it very seldom is a skill; it's just damn luck. It brought to mind the mental picture of an ex-girlfriend who happened to sink one the fourth time she golfed. She wasn't aware of the significance but received accolades and a club trophy. It also gave her years of storytelling. It brought back a memory of a shot I once had of missing a hole-in-one by a millimetre. It just would not drop, no matter how long we waited and jumped about. Maybe, after all, I could do with one. Visions of sinking golf balls danced in my head.

"Okay, let's move!" Mr. Terrific was back, looking quite smug. I wasn't going to ask him why.

I was contrary as I continued to sit and sip. "Tell me, Troy, do you know why I'm here?"

"Because I set you up. I want to finish my game. Once I do, then there'll be no more disappearing golf balls. I'll be happy, the club will be happy, and you'll be too."

"So, you'll tell me where they go and how you do it?"

He was enjoying this far too much. If he had a sleeve, he would be laughing up it.

"Aw, forget it." I sat up straight and returned the Pure Life to its very own holder. "I'll just tell them I haven't a clue." I pushed the bottom button and followed the cart's instructions on reversing and turning.

"No sense of humour, no fun at all."

I drove. Fast!

"Okay, okay! Stop! Let's get straightened out here!"

I stopped. I waited. The magnificent cart queried my decision.

"I did it to stick it to those bastards. They made things hard for me no matter how well I played, no matter how much publicity I gave them. Now, I just want to finish that terrific game. I'll tell you how I make those long shots disappear, but how you explain it to the club is your job."

"And I get a hole-in-one?"

"And you get a hole-in-one. You can have my terrific set of clubs to boot."

"Hell, no! As I said before, I don't want your damn clubs!"

At the H and D words, Troy flinched and I heard the singe-sizzle once more. It did my mean streak good.

"You have to use my clubs when you play the full game, though. You have to get to them and do that."

"I'm a detective. I detect." Oh, how confident I once again felt.

"Let's get to the fifteenth, Mr. Detect. I'll tell you a story on the way."

Once more, the intelligent cart turned me about and we headed off to the fifteenth. The story was quite incredible.

"I have been bestowed with a strong energy field."

The devil, you say, was my thought without interrupting him.

"I don't care to see anyone hitting a perfect long shot as I did. That was my last hurrah." He was showing his malicious side in the telling. "I have the strength to pick a ball up and carry it a fair distance. What confuses them is the bunker shots. They can see the roll line in the sand and then nothing. You should see the dumb looks on their faces and hear their dumb ideas."

As we approached a rise on leaving the fourteenth green, he drew my attention to the scene below. "Look down there;

you get an overall view. See the bush and tall trees in the forest to the right of the course?"

I followed his direction and took in the spectacular outline of the undisturbed forest that surrounded the course. I was aware this Troy Terrific spirit would not be able to venture off the course, so this should be interesting.

"I carry the ball up to the edge of the course. No one can see the ball floating in the air by itself from where they are. Once at the edge, I throw it as far as I can. Now, if you look closely through the trees, mostly in the springtime, you might see a fast-running creek. The beavers have built a dam on the side of it.

"Now, here's the part you won't believe; I didn't at first. Old Daddy Beaver must have been a golfer in a past life, as he has become quite attached to the golf balls I throw his way. He gathers them, one at a time, in his oversized buck teeth and carries them down to his underwater den. He must have quite a collection by now."

As his story came to an end, I reached the back of the fifteenth green. Circling, I was able to see the farthest point of the course he had indicated. I extracted one of the complimentary golf balls, exited my magnificent borrowed buggy, and stepped into the overgrown bush.

"Watch out for snakes!" he called out much too cheerfully.

It wasn't easy going, making my way through the overgrown raspberry bushes and fallen rotten tree limbs. Rather than snakes, my fear was poison ivy. A suit, tie, and leather-soled shoes, worn to impress Manager and Pro, was simply not the best wear for bramble stomping. Fortunately, not too far in, I heard the singing sound of free-running water. After a few more uncertain wobbles and clutching onto low-hanging branches, lo and behold, I spotted a beaver dam in the making. I did not approach, as I was aware of the skittish nature of the flat-tailed rodents. I threw the golf ball ahead of me a little and waited. I am good at waiting.

It took a while, but it was not an unpleasant wait. I heard an echoing goodbye call from the fifteenth. Troy Terrific had finally run out of energy; I could do without him.

Shortly thereafter, the soft rustle of dead leaves and the occasional snap of a twig caught my attention. As sure as no lies were told, I spotted a fat beaver waddling his way cautiously toward the golf ball. His radar was fixed on it. I watched with fascination as he used his front paws with dexterity to pick up the ball, roll it around for comfort, and place it under his front teeth. Satisfied with his placement, he turned about and headed back to his den. With a slap of his tail, I witnessed the disappearance of both beaver and ball!

I waited some more, and then with less finesse than he, I made my way to the edge of the creek and looked down into the weed-streaked running water. As I bent forward, it was possible to make out the intertwining branches and intricate architecture known only to beaver builders. Securing the twigs at the foundation dotted along in formation was a series of round, smooth dimpled objects that once had been white. Wow! How clever was that!

I made my way back to the magnificent cart and let it take me back to the clubhouse. I met once more with Manager and Pro and alluded to the fact that I had a clue or two but needed to play a round. They informed me they could work me into a foursome as a special guest in their upcoming in-house tournament. That gave me two weeks to practise and nervously ponder my wisdom. Golfing with the comradery of my buddies is one thing, but how small would I shrivel under the scrutiny of semi-pros? I doubted they would be kind. The arrogance of Troy Terrific would no doubt shine through and they wouldn't like me. No, not one bit.

———

Two weeks later, I found myself once more stopped along the lovely entrance to the Trails Golf Club. Troy Terrific was waiting at the same spot, looking just as arrogant and overconfident as ever.

"I can't waste energy on you" was his "*Good morning, how are you?*" "The lock code is left twelve, right thirty-five, twice round left fifteen, right forty. Don't mess up." And *poof*! He was gone.

I sang the code in my head to the tune of "We Will Rock You." Maybe that way I would remember it.

It was a bit of a back and forth with Jim the Pro, convincing him I had forgotten my clubs and needed to borrow a set of TaylorMades if they had an extra lying around. He was a busy man this early A.M. He was, and rightly so, peeved, disgusted, and fed up with me and what he thought were my demanding idiosyncrasies. He left me with the shopkeep to see what he could do for me.

"Not much," he retorted in a "who cares anyway" attitude. "You can buy a set." He eyed me with a sneer. "The only full set I know of belonged to a former member, and they're locked in his locker and no one has the lock combination."

"I'm a detective. I can detect."

He showed me the way to the locker room and waited. Like when thieves break into a safe in a movie, I made a show of placing my ear close to the dial as I turned it slowly, listening for the click. *We will* . . . left twelve . . . *we will* . . . right thirty-five . . . *rock you* . . . twice around. The lock pulled down. I opened the door, and there was Troy Terrific's pristine set of clubs surrounded in precise order, along with all the regalia that goes with the game, from caps, gloves, tees to bug spray.

"I just need the clubs," I informed him as I pulled them out by the back strap. "I'll go out to the driving range and hit a few." He just nodded and watched as I shut the locker door but did not lock up.

I kept to myself with head down, first on the driving range and then on the putting green. Troy did not make an appearance. I couldn't read that one way or another. My nervousness was starting to hit a new high. I waited until most of the other practicing members were on their way to the clubhouse for their instructions before I left too. Jim Pro was assigning the foursomes to their carts and designated starting holes. My foursome was to start on the first. *This is a setup*, I thought.

I introduced myself and shook their hands, even though they showed great reluctance. I loaded the bag onto the passenger side of the cart I was assigned. They didn't express great joy to have me in their group. I didn't query how the score would be kept or what handicap I was given. Just speak when I must and keep smiling was my plan. *Troy Terrific, enter at your leisure.*

As the newbie with a given handicap and as Pro's guest, I was the fourth to tee off. It was very intimidating as I watched my team hit beautiful tee shots. They then moved back to watch me, along with the usual crowd that had gathered from the clubhouse at the start of the tournament. Many cameras and cell phones were held high.

Silence reigned. I had broken an unspoken rule before I had even begun: I was not ready. I stood there watching and had not donned my glove, picked out a tee, or selected my club. All was still on the cart. *Keep calm and carry on, slooowly. Pick up that Troy Terrific attitude. The world owes me a living. They won't like me anyway.*

I ambled over to the cart, pulled a glove on my left hand, and velcroed it tightly, then reached for a tee—any tee would do—and a club ball, noting the number on it. As I unzipped the golf bag, I heard Terrific's voice: "A glove on your left hand? But you're left-handed!"

I put him on ignore once more. He'd figure it out soon.

I reached for the driver, ready to strip off its pristine cover. I felt a cold electric current enter the back of my neck, run through both arms and down the length of my spine. My left arm was suspended in mid-air as Troy took control, and in a patronizing tone I hadn't heard him use before, he informed me, "Not the driver, use the three wood. Stay to the right. I'll par this hole just like I did before."

Have you ever been heavily sedated or had the feeling of walking through a tunnel with exaggerated motion? Perhaps you could relate to Popo the Puppet, who can do anything as long as somebody pulls the strings. The meaning or purpose is somewhere beyond you. You are in control, but then again you are not. Then again, it doesn't matter.

I was not me as I teed up, stepped back, looked down the fairway, checked out the right side, took two practice swings, approached with an arrogant shake of the club, addressed the ball, and swung. It . . . felt . . . perfect!!! It was perfect!!!

The crowd reacted favourably. The electric jolt left my body like a garden hose trickling slowly to a stop. I was once more me, standing alone, watching the other three loading into the carts. *Move*, I told myself. I quickly scurried over to the back of the cart, returned the club to its spot in the bag, and hopped in.

My driving partner said not a word, nor did he notice Troy hanging on to the top handle grip as he rode sidestep along with us. I wondered where Troy had picked up his green logoed cap and a black golf glove. He did not have them with him when we met before, and I knew he couldn't go shopping. I refrained from asking, but as I touched the brim of my cap and pulled at my glove wrist, he understood. "Keep them in my back pockets," he muttered.

When the silent driver stopped for my approach shot, I heard, felt, but did not see: "You are a right-handed player, aren't you? Thanks for nothing. It's not nice to mess with my kind. Use the nine iron. I'll land it just in front of the green." He slid again into my being and had me reach for said iron. Even when one knows the cold shock is coming, one tenses, waiting.

A chip and a putt gave me the foretold par. My silent cart partner seemed somewhat impressed as did I and condescended to hand me a scorecard. He filled me in on the club scoring procedure. I humbly thanked him.

While waiting to tee off on the second hole, I backed off a little to have a chat with Mr. T. Terrific. "Are you going to jump in and out and give a play-by-play for every shot? I don't think I have the physical stamina for this. Can't you just stay and shut up?"

His response was quick and rather insulting. "I don't have the energy to stay in between shots. I need most of my energy for the fifteenth and on. No more commentary; that will help. Now that I know I don't have to juice up your left arm, that will help too. Anything else you're holding back?"

I shook my head in the negative while looking at the clubs, hoping to convince my partner I was making a big decision on selection.

"Just relax and make like a zombie. Wherever did you get the idea I was enjoying your body anyway?"

Was a hole-in-one worth this abuse? When would he bestow this promise upon me? It would have to be after the fifteenth.

By the time we golfed our way to the tee box on the fifteenth, I had gained some respect from my mates. My score and modesty had won them over. They were not aware I felt like a drainage ditch, with all the filling up and pouring out of Terrific stuff.

"This hole is haunted," our captain informed me in an intimidating way. If he expected me to ask for clarification, he was disappointed, but he carried on regardless. "One of our members died here right after he hit a long second shot. Guess he put too much energy into it. His heart gave out, and they carried him off dead, or dying anyway. Ever since that happened, no one has been able to hit a long shot up to the front of the green. Some of us take up the challenge, though. It can play with your psyche, depending on whether you believe in ghost stories or not."

They all gave an embarrassing chuckle and turned to the drives at hand. An extra surge of angry determination seemed to accompany my next spiritual bolt. If Troy allowed this wimp to get to his ego, we may be doomed.

I had the honour of teeing first, and it was a beaut. Troy was about to do damage to my biceps. Wimp was next and made like an Alice. My fairway shot was long, and Troy landed it right where he had ended his game and his life. My partners verified this was so. They also verified my ball may not be there when I approached. I could only remain silent.

Of course, there it was, to their amazement, right where it should be.

Troy stayed with me now to play the holes he had not finished. He had become actively serious and obnoxious.

"Listen up: This is uphill with the green sloping forward. I need to hit high and let it run back. Let's go with the eight." He had me reach for it. I had no reason nor desire to challenge his choice or attitude. I did want to ask about the impending hole-in-one, but instead did his bidding and became his puppet on a string once more.

I tuned him out as he gave a play-by-play of what he would do and then what he did do. He was having the time of his spiritual form. I roboted along, smiling and nodding in response to anything and everything my partners verbalized in my direction. Troy was ecstatic to have racked up a par not only on the fifteenth, but also going forward to the eighteenth. He hovered over my shoulder, blowing his frigid breath down my neck whilst our scorecards were being verified. He had thirty-four on the front nine and likewise on the back, totalling four under par. There were mixed feelings all around about me.

I excused myself to return Troy's clubs to his locker, change my shoes, and throw a little water on my person. Troy did not make an appearance. I could only assume he had spent his full tank of energy. That was just fine with me for now, but I needed reassurance about getting my payment.

When I returned to the conference room, drinks were flowing while the score results were being displayed on overhead monitors. My name was bobbing about in the top three as percentages were worked out.

I became aware my presence was drawing attention. Who was this newbie with a great score? How did he get in here? Is he a plant? Could he be allowed to take our trophies?

I held my head high and decided to fake Terrific. Jim Pro and Manager looked like they were being bombarded with questions that demanded answers, mostly from the golfers who usually took club honours. As soon as they spied me, they broke ranks and headed my way. They caught up as I was ordering my drink and telling the keep to put it and the tip on Manager's tab.

Jim Pro got right to the riot-rousing matter at hand. "You told us you were a weekend warrior. If you wanted to make us look like fools, you've done a hell of a good job."

I smelled burning and heard an evil cackle. Revenge, thy name is Troy the Terrible.

Stick to the truth as much as possible. I lowered my head in a humble pose and began apologetically, "Truthfully, I have to tell you something. I was so taken with your hospitality and feeling so intimidated about my lousy golf, I have been taking serious lessons and getting out on a course as much as I can. I wasn't aware an in-depth effort could make such a difference. I suppose I should have told you I was trying to improve my game to impress you. I am so sorry, guys. I don't want to be on your scoreboard. Can you remove my single at least? I know it has to stay there for the partner score. Maybe you can fudge the large handicap you allotted me. That wasn't fair, was it?" I looked as pained as I could, knowing my three partners would want to keep that score intact. I was all for letting them sort it out. Manager quickly skipped to the next item on the agenda. "You hit a long shot on the fifteenth and your ball stayed there. Have you solved that mystery?"

Redemption was at hand. "Yes, I have." They both perked up. "After dinner, can we go out? I'll introduce you to the problem."

They were all for squeezing answers out of me right there and then, but club members swooped around on all sides, demanding answers for their hurt egos. They were petted and compensated and became less disgruntled when it was announced as a visiting guest, I would have recognition only and be given a complimentary eighteen-hole game with cart and lunch any day between Monday and Thursday in October with Jim Pro as my partner and any two others that signed up first to play with us. My partners in this tournament were informed there had been an error when assigning my handicap, as I had never registered with Golf Ontario. They agreed to chop it substantially, but not to the point of losing the tournament.

All was fair in love and golf. Whew!

─────

It was nearing twilight when we as a trio carted out to the far side of the fifteenth green. I mentioned they might consider bringing along a flashlight or two just in case. I did not enlighten them about what "just in case" meant. Adding a little mysterious wonder may salvage my detection reputation, as my golf reputation was dubious at best.

As we reached the edge of the property line, I stopped the cart, disembarked, and beckoned them to follow me. "We have to do a little bush treading," I told them. "Just keep behind me."

Manager, putting hands on hips, was skeptical. "Are you sure you know what you're doing?"

O ye of little faith! "Just come along, this won't take long. Got your flashlights?" I sounded as upbeat as I could. Our little line was moving right along with Jim behind me and Manager bringing up the rear.

"Watch out for snakes!" The devil made me say it! They both stood stalk still. "Come on. We're almost there." I felt almost Terrible.

I compensated by trying to hold the raspberry brambles back for them, but I only succeeded in letting them go in time to swat them both across their person. I left them to their own devices at the same time I heard the familiar babble of the brook.

"Here we are!" I announced softly. "Step over here. Careful now. Shine your lights down at the bottom of those twigs. That's right. Now, tell me what you see."

They both looked and were bug-eyed and mesmerized.

"Well, my God!" was Pro's reaction, while Manager just appeared stupefied. "That's a beaver dam glorified with our golf balls. Is that the culprit that has caused the disappearance of the balls?"

"That would be the cause, Jim. Now, how you remedy the cause is the problem for you to solve. I only detect." With that, I turned about, and they stumbled around to follow me back to the carts.

When we reached the carts, Manager finally spoke and questioned, "How then, would we see the roll line of the ball in the sand and then it, too, would disappear?"

I did have an explanation I was hoping not to use, but there it was, needed. I raised my arms slightly, palms up, and was most patronizing. "You live up here in this wonderful area, sir, so I expect you understand the tale of the beaver tail. It is flat and broad and he drags it behind him, doesn't he? Nature has bestowed this wonderfulness upon him to outwit his enemies. You see, as he picks the ball up from the bunker and leaves, that tail wipes out all signs of entry and exit as he waddles back from whence he came. Now nature has also bestowed upon him a coat of multi-browns that blends into his surroundings so no one is eagle-eyed enough to spot him. He didn't take the close-up golf shots, as the golfers were closing in, and beavers are, as I am sure you know, too timid to venture forth." I was sticking to the truth in a fanciful way, wasn't I?

Marshall pulled a face full of serious thought and held it for a minute in time while Jim and I waited.

He relaxed somewhat and made his proclamation. "Of course, of course. Our members will be relieved to have the disappearances solved. The problem will be rectified once we call a board meeting and get some input into a solution, won't it, Jim." It sounded to me like a warning, not a request. I believe Jim got the message.

I made an effort to join my buddies for their weekly games. They referred to themselves as the Ragtag Swingers. I was getting into the swing of things both literally and figuratively, enjoying the game now that I had more understanding, confidence, and, therefore, success with this silly psychological game. I even allowed them to sign me up as part of their team to enter a tournament later in the season at the Taboo Muskoka Golf Course, a prestigious course with the reputation of being tourist friendly. It was close to my cottage, so it offered an excuse to entertain my buddies for the weekend. My weekly games were keeping my swing rhythm going for my upcoming promised October game at the Trails Golf Club. This, I expected but was not sure, was when Troy

Terrific Black would come through with my coveted hole-in-one. I even splurged on a few new essential clubs and practised as time permitted down at the Docks.

Working along the telephone line of "I know a guy that knows a guy and he said . . .", it wasn't long before my Trails Club adventure and upcoming October visit was known among my buddies, with a few extra exciting tidbits thrown in for the telling. Could they come too and play a round with me? No! Could they come to watch? No! I would arrange to have them barred. Well, then, they would wait for the Barrie CTV news to announce the exciting results. Sometimes, it's best not to have friends at all!

The drive to the Trails on the early October morning of my big day was spectacular. The autumn leaves of red and gold had spent their beauty and were swirling to the ground in whirls made by those gulps of wind that spring up on their own accord. The maples and birches were being stripped naked, allowing the pines room to display their limbs to their fullest. I drove at an even pace up Highway 27, allowing vehicles to pass when they could. No worries . . . yet.

As I entered the golf grounds, lo and behold, Troy Terrific was waiting as before. The difference was telling. He was even more agitated than before and had a darker scowl. I lowered my window as he growled at me. "I told you to take my clubs. It wouldn't have hurt you at all. Now, look at them."

"And good morning to you too! Taking your clubs would have been stealing—not a big habit of mine. Why should they matter to you now anyway? Been there, done that, game over. Your turn to give the promised payment, then I'm out of here."

"My clubs are in the shop on sale for less than fifty percent of what they are worth. Everyone knows they are mine, so they won't buy them. They're like a shrine, being held like a memorial. I'm not liking that. All my other golf things, including those marvellous expensive shoes, were dumped. That's just insulting. I need you to go and buy my clubs, NOW. Then you won't have stolen them."

He does indeed know how to raise the fluff and feathers even after his demise. "Troy, listen up now. I don't need nor want your clubs. I have some new ones that are just fine. Stay with me today for my payment, and then we're done. Got it?"

His eyes danced with danger. I felt the warnings of a deal gone dead. I knew it was wrong to trust a spirit; they are so arrogant and needy. He raised his arms and clenched his fists. I felt the chill reach in through my window. The urge to close it was overridden by the need to keep the locked stare with him and get the promise paid.

His voice sounded echoing and threatening as I heard, "Did I promise you payment today?" He smiled a crooked, evil smile. His white teeth sparkled.

The horn blasting from the car on my tail jerked me back to reality and whisked him away in a whirlwind of red and gold leaves.

Was I shaken? You betcha!

I recognized immediately the loophole in our agreement. I had not nailed down the day, time, or game when he would give me my payment. He, as a spirit, would not be able to leave the area of his last earthly being. I was fairly certain I would not be back to the Trails another time. I could only move forward as if I knew he would make good on the payment today.

I dropped my clubs off at the bag rack, proceeded to the parking lot, changed my shoes, and went to the clubhouse to search for my partners. As I walked up the stone steps to the glass double doors, Troy Terrific made his last appeal. He walked backwards in front of me, ensuring his evil air enveloped me with every forward motion and breath I took. "Last chance. My clubs are in the shop. Turn right. Go! Get! Them!"

"Oh, there you are, Detective." Jim the Pro was cheerful enough as he approached. With spiritual unawareness, he walked straight to me, passing through Terrific's space. He stopped, then rolled his shoulders forward in a shudder. "Getting chilly in here already. Have to turn the heat on soon." Terrific turned away in a mist, giving me a sideway slant of his burning blue eyes.

I will mercifully spare you the details of my game, except to let you know I anticipated Troy to control me each time we approached one of the four par three holes. He did not. Not a vision nor a sound came forth from the other side to honour the promissory bargain. He welched, and I was on my own. My partners were anticipating greater than I gave, but from my view of my game, I performed better than I thought I would. Acceptable for a Ragtag, but where was the love from the private membership golfers? I begged off the nineteenth hole drink, lunch, and replay of the game and exited the way I had entered. Troy Terrific Black did not materialize. His anger at not succeeding in reaching into the physical world to control the ownership of his clubs must have been so great, that he was willing to renege on his promise. This was something he would have to deal with in his domain, and something I would have to rack up to a lesson learned. I knew I needed to be careful with the spirits, and I could blame no one but myself for allowing me to be lulled in by a promise to boost my ego. *C'est la vie.*

I arrived at my cottage a day or two before the Ragtag tournament to make sure it was housekeeping clean and I had a chance to make the necessary trips to load up on groceries and refreshments. When everything was in order for the after tournament celebration, I took myself off to the Taboo Muskoka course. After an introduction, I requested some time on the driving range.

With my new clubs and confidence, I snared a cart and found my way to the sloping, granite-rock driving range. Driving a ball down into the valley below gave the illusion of an extraordinarily long drive. Only the markers dashed the dream. Muskoka chairs were placed strategically at each side with the expectation that one may have to wait during busy times. This was one of them. I extracted my driver and three wood, undressed them, located a couple of tees and a glove, and slipped down into a brightly painted yellow chair.

My aura must have slipped as well without the usual lightheaded notice. She appeared to the right of me, hands on hips, watching the less-than-competent weekend warriors swing their clubs with killer force. She was dressed for a game: a powder blue sports top with a zipper front stopping at a pull-up collar; short sleeves sporting the embroidered club name; matching plaid skort stopping above her knees; and blue-saddled white golf shoes. She wasn't young. She looked weathered by the sun and rough weather days on the course. Her skin, though wrinkled, was still muscle firm. Her grey-streaked hair was shoulder length and held behind her ears with a dark blue visor.

I waited. She spoke. "Most of those guys have no idea how to use their legs. They seem to think they just have to swing fast. I hope you don't do that."

"I did once." I paused and dove right in. "Why are you here?"

She crouched down as one does when getting the line on a putt. "I don't have a request. I'm here to help you."

I've been down that road before with disastrous results. "No help needed with anything, thank you very much."

A tee box became vacant, so I stood and started toward it.

She stopped me with "A promise made is a debt unpaid. Troy Black is ostracized and burning in hell for welching on his promise. I have been sent to rectify the situation and bestow upon you the hole-in-one as per the contract."

By the time I hesitated and turned toward her, the empty tee box was no longer empty. Another weekend warrior had bumped the line.

I pulled out my cell and put it to my ear, the trick I had learned to not look maniacal. "Walk with me." I was definitely interested, although Troy Terrific burning in hell did tickle my fancy.

"I am a spirit, not a ghost. I can only roam about the golf course and where the accompanied nine-hole course used to be. That is fine with me; I love it here. I had a hole-in-one here not long after the course opened. It was on the eleventh. It has changed somewhat since then, but I have been observant since I received word this was my mission. It is doable just as I did it, if you allow me to take control just as you did with Troy. I don't have the strength that Troy had, so you must be very pliable."

The thought of having an elderly woman enter my being and taking control was not appealing. No, not at all. I was macho enough to wonder if I would condescend if she was young and beautiful.

With that thought in mind, I was ashamed of myself. "Lay it out for me," I encouraged her.

"I belonged to the ladies' group. We played at the nine-hole Sands Course. We called ourselves The Red Tees. We played in tournaments held by other clubs and sponsored our own. If there was a special rate here at Taboo, we would make up foursomes and then have dinner at the hotel afterward. We kept handicaps with Golf Ontario and took part in some of their activities. As you know, a hole-in-one is never planned. You hope to get on the green as close to the hole as possible on a par three. Sometimes, luck comes along. I used an eight iron; not sure why. It clipped high and flew over the water at a side angle, then rolled back and in. I got cheers all around, and they had drinks on me. Are you ready for that?"

Sure, I was. A foursome, four drinks including me ... worth at least one hole-in-one after my initial disappointment.

"I'm all for it," I told her as I turned heel and headed back along the path toward the driving range once more. She stayed with me. "Are you sure you can do this?" I then quickly added in an effort not to insult her advanced years. "If the course has changed since your hole-in-one, maybe your technique will be like before, but the hole layout won't be."

I don't believe she bought it for a moment, but she gracefully responded, "Better to have tried and failed than not have tried at all. What have you got to lose anyway, besides control of your physical being to a woman for a short spell in your lifetime." She smiled a wry smile and added, "I daresay you have done that more times than you would care to admit."

Had she been peeking into my past?

I ignored her wryness and got right to the point. "Let's give it a try then. We start our Ragtag tournament this Saturday at nine a.m. You will be watching, I assume, and ready to take over on the eleventh when my foursome arrives there?"

"Correct," she answered faintly.

A tee box opened up; I hastened forward in time to claim it. "Want to jump me and have a practice right now?" I asked.

"Can't. I'm used up." And wearily she faded away.

I did receive an interesting questioning look from the man in the tee box on my right that I did not return.

Saturday proved to be a rather brisk day with a gusty wind and the temperature low enough to make one keep the golf jacket zippered up and gloves on both hands. The leaves danced about to a tune of their own, making leaf pickups on the greens a necessity. This did not bode well for a ball that needed to roll long and into a hole, but as my spirit gal proclaimed, it was to be or not to be. What did I have to lose but my bodily functions, golfwise that is.

Anticipation grew with each stroke. I needed to breathe deeply and slowly. The cool wind made it difficult to determine if she was about or not. I thought not, as she indicated her strength would be minimal and needed for the upcoming deed.

We were playing ready golf, so I was prepared to be not ready as we approached the eleventh tee. I waited in the cart, caressing my trusty eight iron. She appeared beside me wearing her blue outfit and looking not the least bit chilly.

"Let's go, Tiger." She smiled. "Celebrity time!"

I had no answer for that bit of sarcasm. Control was already lost. I was scarcely aware of the tee movement and chatter of my team, but fully aware of the electrical charge as she entered by the preferred method. The back of my neck tingled. Oh, how that makes me shudder! The jolt travelled down my spine and along the length of my arms and legs all in one fell swoop. Immediately, I felt girlish.

My walk up to the tee box was slow with short steps. I felt my hips swaying and my shoulders dipping in an unfamiliar motion. She had me bend one knee to place the tee while holding the club and ball upright in my right hand. I was ready to rise when she spoke.

"Too high. Lower the tee right down to ground level." I did that in a fussy girlish manner.

We stood and held the club out in front of us and pointed it toward the green. A gust of wind blew a lock of hair across our face. A shake of our head did not remove it, so we placed the club in front of our legs, leaning it on our stomach. With both hands, we twisted our hair behind our ears, locked it there with the dark blue visor, and then smoothed it down.

I was aware somewhere in the depths of my being, my partners were silent, bug-eyed, and slack-jawed at my movements. I relaxed and let her do what she willed.

She placed the club precisely in my hands, thumbs aligned, took a couple of knee bends, club head behind the ball, wiggled my bum, no practice swing, and unloaded.

That little white sphere rose into the wind. We watched as it caught air and sailed upward and right on over the green.

She put my hand over my mouth and I giggled. "Oh no, oh golly! Too much club for the wind."

The golf gods are fickle, aren't they? The ball hit ground and suffered a knock on its logo from a concealed water tap and ricocheted back onto the green. It began a fast roll backward, but not in line with the hole. Where was a beaver when you needed one? Just as sure as golf balls are made in China, this one was skimming past the designated hole when—be it a wind gust controlling a maple leaf or my ghost gal whipping up a whirl, I didn't know—that ball developed one thought in mind and I liked it. It abruptly turned left... and... it... sunk! Leaves went fluttering on by.

I realized my body was limp and I was me once more. She was gone. My buddies were pounding on me. That's no way to treat a lady, so I was surely thankful she had taken an early departure.

We shouted and jumped about as only the joy of a hole-in-one can bring. Drinks on the nineteenth were declared! My foursome was already placing their order. Cell phones were spreading the word of my accomplishment. They ribbed me about the help of a water tap and a maple leaf. I knew more jest would follow, but this would live in Ragtag infamy.

I approached the clubhouse feeling terrific, taking the congratulations in high style. Have you ever seen or heard of a modest hole-in-oner?

My balloon burst shortly after drinks were ordered. The barkeep pulled me aside to inform me my card was declined, as it was maxed out.

What? How could this be? "Well," he informed me, "there are forty guys in your tournament group. They're drinking the good stuff, and they think the word drink has an S on the end."

9 DOWN BY THE RIVERSIDE

THE FIRST TIME I saw her, I was just mildly surprised. I had expected to find a presence there at the bend in the river. What amazed me was the fact she was a she and so young. My first glance suggested she was about the age of eight or ten.

I found her sitting dangerously close to the edge of the embankment. She could easily slide into the river and that, I expect, was how she had met her demise. She had her knees up supporting the book she was reading. She looked up over the book and gave me a huge grin as if she had been expecting me. Her brown hair was cut short, hanging just below her ears. Her full bangs were cut evenly across her forehead. A sprinkling of freckles ran across her cheeks and her upturned nose.

I seldom go looking for ghosts and never for spirits; in fact, I do my best to avoid them. But the rumour around the town of Bracebridge concerning the bend in the river at this juncture piqued my curiosity. And so on this sunny afternoon, I took a canoe trip down from the town dock just below the Silver Bridge Falls, then under the bridge at Wellington Street and out the north branch to the bend in the river.

While a couple of trade paperback books have been published on the localities of buildings that are deemed to be haunted, none have included this mysterious current in the river. The building haunts are aimed more, in my humble opinion, to gain the attention of the summer tourists and collect them together for a midnight walk through the designated old spots for a fun fright night, for a fee, of course.

The mystery river current at this particular spot was experienced in broad daylight if the canoeists or those in a small watercraft found themselves too close to the north shoreline. It happened for no scientific reason. They would suddenly find themselves being pushed sideways out into the middle of the river. No matter how hard the occupants tried to paddle against this driving force, it was to no avail. Once they were in the middle they could then continue with their journey.

Victims of this shared their stories, warning others to stay away from that spot. Some took care to hug the middle of the river as they passed the bend, while the adventurists purposely sought it out to prove the account.

Stories sprung up adding to the eeriness. The dark waters of the Muskoka rivers are due to the runoff of the cedar and pine, but who knows what lurks below? Perhaps a powerful force waits to be explained.

And so it was that I relaxed the weak side of my aura and welcomed in whatever wanted to show itself to me. A young girl could not be an unholy spirit, or could she?

As I sat in the canoe, with my paddle out of the water and resting across the canoe's centre, I was aware I was not being pushed sideways out into the middle of the river as the tale forewarned—I was not moving at all. The forward current that should have taken me ahead was not.

I finally spoke. "I didn't think you'd be so young."

"It's not that I'm all that young, it's because you are old." Her grin grew even wider.

How bold she was. I wasn't that old. An arm stretch to forty isn't old, is it? Well, to a young girl, I suppose it is. I had a feeling I wasn't going to like her, but my curiosity was bigger than my dislike.

She closed her book, raised one hip, and slid it under her bottom. She had no trouble with that movement. She was wearing jeans and a T-shirt. I was not privy to the reason she was only wearing one sneaker. She wrapped her arms around her raised knees and settled down as if she was preparing for a dialogue. She waited.

I found myself at a disadvantage. Usually, it was the visitors from this other realm who sought me out for a reason of their own, and the control was mine. Here, I was seeking out an answer to the mystifying river current and from a young girl, no less. I had never communicated with a child before. I didn't have anything in common with young people. I didn't know any of them.

"How old are you?"

"Ten."

I was spot on with that. "Is it you that's causing the canoes and boats to move sideways into the middle of the river?"

"Yep."

"Why?"

"'Cause I want to."

"Why?"

"'Cause, I'm bored."

I was getting nowhere in a hurry with my line of questioning. She was having fun at my expense. "How do you do it?"

"Hang on!" She leaped forward and with no effort, grabbed the side of my canoe with both hands and pushed.

Her body was floating straight out with no leverage behind the push while she acted like a rudder.

I held on to the bar in front of me in time to avoid a wet tumble, as the canoe was turned at a ninety-degree angle and scooted sideways in an impossible way. The swirls around the bow indicated the amount of force that was used.

I sat still in amazement and looked around. The water rippled, birds chirped, and dogs barked. Nothing was out of the ordinary, except for the frigid wind that swirled around me on that hot summer's day as she performed a backward flip over the canoe and me. Suddenly, she was on the other side of my vessel, pushing me back to her shoreline. She dove into a forward somersault over the canoe and landed right back in her sitting position on the grassy bank. She threw back her head and gave a loud, carefree laugh.

Child or adult, I was wise enough to know there was no point in telling her to stop doing this to people going by. She was enjoying the reactions she was getting and had no reason to abandon her fun. I decided I would treat her as I did my adult encounters and see where that got me. I didn't care if she stopped or not; I had already satisfied my curiosity as to how this side of the river was creating its telephone line tales. I would politely tell her goodbye and hope she would allow me to paddle forth.

But instead, I asked, "Are you a ghost or a spirit?"

"A spirit."

Her answer was not what I had expected. How could one so young have gathered up so much negativity in her life to be placed in the realm of nastiness rather than ghostliness?

"Why?"

She was not at all remorseful as she gave me a list of her transgressions during her short time on Earth.

"I liked to steal things. It was fun. I lied a lot ... about anything. I bullied other kids. It was easy with the little twirps. They scare so easy. People believed me when I cried and said I was sorry."

I knew I wouldn't like this kid. How did she get this way? She must have had a family at the time. I had to rein in these thoughts, or I would find myself taking on a dilemma I had no desire to get involved in. She seemed to be quite content with her lot, and the mystery was giving the users of the river folklore to repeat and exaggerate to their liking.

I carried on instead. "How did you end up stuck here? Did you fall in and drown?"

"Yep, I slid right in." She used a flat hand to indicate a slide. "Head first, upside down. I was sitting here, reading my sister's diary. I had stolen that. I was reading secrets I wasn't supposed to know. I put my legs down, and *zippo*, I did a flip. I grabbed some hanging weeds, but the current here was pretty strong and they just ripped right out of the ground. I remember gulping a lot of water.

"They didn't find me until the next day. I had been carried all the way down to where the river forks. That's where it slows. They never did find out I came from here. Not very good detectives, were they?"

"Doesn't it bother you that your life was cut so early? You didn't have a chance to grow up."

She hugged her knees and rocked back and forth—no wonder she fell in. "No, I would have ruined more lives, I suppose. I was a bad apple to begin with, and I liked causing trouble. I would have ended up here anyway. Well, not on this very spot, but maybe somewhere worse."

She stopped rocking, put her hands on the ground, bent forward, and addressed me seriously. "You can help me with that."

"I think you have mistaken me for someone who cares," I told her. "I have no interest in why, how, or what you do here. I was just curious about why small crafts were being pushed out into the middle of the river. Now I know why, so I'll move along. Nice to have met you. Keep doing what you're doing. You're having fun, and the locals love passing the lore on to the tourists."

Set to turn out into the river, I dug my paddle underwater when she suddenly lurched forward and stopped me with a two-handed hold on the side of the vessel.

"I'll keep you here until you hear what I want to say and do what I want you to do."

She wasn't my first spirit, and as I had decided to treat the situation as if she were an adult, I recognized the symptoms and was able to respond.

"Your voice is becoming an echo, and you're becoming see-through. All those acrobatic leaps have taken most of your energy. There's nothing left to bully with, little girl. You'll soon have to let go of my canoe and me."

With that, she trailed off, and a slight mist receded to the shore and my trusty canoe set its rightful course out along nature's true current.

I carried on with my work at CODA for another couple of weeks before I was able to return to Muskoka again. That little girl spirit entered my mind at least once a day. I wondered about her family and how long ago she had met her watery grave. Her apparel of the T-shirt sporting only the script of MUSKOKA and a pair of jeans were standard for her age and in style forever. Her one sneaker had me guessing, though. Where was the other one?

She hadn't appeared to be at all stressed with her situation. She had told me she was enjoying watching and waiting for unsuspecting voyagers. I wondered if she pulled them into her shore as well as pushed them out. I was doing a psychological number on myself, and my curiosity was growing.

I knew I would soon have to take my canoe along the north branch of the river once more and slow down at that bend. I told myself I just wanted to ask a few questions about her family and why she had to continuously read her sister's diary, but deep down, I knew I was fooling myself. I also wanted to know what she needed help with, but then, would I be able to demand payment if I did the asking? I was good at playing the waiting game. I could wait until she did the asking. What kind of payment could a little girl spirit provide? No sense in avoiding the situation I had talked myself into. This coming weekend would find me heading north on Highway 11.

Saturday was overcast with a steady wind that blew across the river in an easterly direction. I wasn't sure if this would interfere with the girl's ability to play tugboat or not. There was little traffic on the river as I paddled forth, so I surmised she would be bored. With a few questions in mind, I nosed my Langford over to the bend and watched the overgrown bushes for any change in the wind's behaviour or temperature.

I didn't have long to wait, as there she was, knees up, book propped just so, and grin as large as the Cheshire Cat's while she gave me her "I knew you would be back so I win" attitude.

I waded right in. "How about you tell me your name? How long have you been here? Don't you think your parents miss you and grieve for you? Why do you have to keep reading your sister's diary? A kid your age couldn't have been all that nasty. You wouldn't have had time to learn horrible tricks."

"What's it to you?" she retorted. "You don't need to know that stuff. My family's big, crooked liars anyways."

She gave a sniff and wiped her nose with an upward push of the heel of her hand. "People are sad for themselves when someone dies 'cause they miss them for themselves. It's their feelings that are hurt."

She embraced the diary to her chest and mimicked the sound of a grieving mother. "*Oh, how could you do this to ME! Oh, I'LL miss you! Oh, I'M heartbroken!*'"

I was dumbstruck! *What a brat!* I thought. She had no feelings or emotional ties to those left to mourn her.

My background holds no knowledge of what the average ten-year-old is like; therefore, I had no norm to gauge her. I waited.

She rested the diary once more on her knees. "I want you to help me do something good." She lowered her head but raised her eyes in a "pretty please" type of look—that, I recognized as a standard look common of most females.

"There is a payment for the help I give; I think you know that. No freebies or discounts. Even for kids under twelve." I wanted to set the ground rules before listening to what I expected would be a sob story.

"I don't know how I can pay you. What do you want? I don't have anything or know anybody that can give you anything."

I maintained my toughness. "Well, I don't want to hear about what you want until you think of a payment. I'll check in with you another day."

I pushed the edge of my paddle against the riverbank and backed out into the river. She made no effort to stop me. If a little girl spirit could pout, she was pouting.

I carried on down the river, keeping slightly over on the right side. Rules of the road apply to the river as well. Due to the fact there was little river traffic that day, I was able to go slow and take in the natural scenery as well as the cottages, boats with their custom shelters, and older homes updated with pride.

On this route, the narrow roads continue along the river on both sides. The north road takes you to Santa's Village: Santa's summer home on the forty-fifth parallel has been a memory maker for four generations of believers. Whereas, the south road takes you well beyond the boundaries of the town and past the Old Stage Coach Road, still in use but kept a secret by its regular travellers.

Just before I reached the fork in the branch of the river, I ruddered back and reversed my path back to the town dock. My tranquil ride had done wonders for my soul, to use the term loosely, and I was determined to keep to the opposite side of the river as I approached the bend again, but my eyes wanted to look across, searching for a flicker of misty movement that was beyond the realm of most.

A good plan it was, and my eyes did indeed catch a movement. I surmised she was not able to make the journey over to the far side of the river; halfway seemed to be the property line for her.

She was standing and jumping up and down, waving her arms in the air. She looked like she was in full exercise mode.

I relented, leisurely stroking my way across. As I did, she assumed her original position of sitting down, with her knees up, held together by her arms.

She waited until I nosed into the bank before she made her announcement in a loud triumphant manner. One would have thought she had won Olympic gold.

"I have it!" she declared. "An over-the-top, super-duper, fantastically really great payment for you. This will be a feather on top of your head... or wherever. This will be suspenseful, just like a good mystery should be. Ready? This is what you got to do."

She shifted about and snuggled down on her grassy knoll, preparing to tell me about her payment. Her face was animated. That was quite a feat for a spirit. Usually, they stuck to scowls and growls.

She raised one hand and one pointer finger. "First of all, what day is it today?"

"Saturday."

"Okay, then. You need to be here early Wednesday morning."

"I can't. I need to be back in the city at work."

She abruptly raised both arms high in the air and slid forward into the water but remained afloat.

"Oh, for Chr—criminy sake!"

I knew spirits felt burning crispiness if they took the Lord's name in vain, and obviously, she had had a sampling of that.

"Haven't you ever taken a day off work? Besides, wait 'til I tell you my payment. You'll be working for it. Now shut up and listen! Look downstream a little bit."

I did.

"Do you see that clump of birches sticking out over the water?"

I did.

"Well, do you? Answer me."

"You told me to shut up." I couldn't resist that. The devil made me do it.

"Well, nod your head then, smartass. Do you?"

I nodded.

"Go down there and look around at the trees and the landing around it, then come back and tell me what you see. Don't take too long."

I knew she wanted to have control of the situation. I also knew she would have a limited amount of energy to expel. She wasted so much of it by jumping around and showing off. Being so young and new at this, I suppose, she couldn't help it.

I did her bidding and paddled down the thirty metres or so to the bank she had indicated. It was a worn area that appeared to be used as a boat landing or docking, not an unusual sight along this river. Tied to a low-hanging branch of the sturdiest birch tree was a yellow nylon rope. It ran down the length of the trunk to the ground where it was reinforced by U-hooks. It then trailed down the bank and into the water.

I duly detected all details and returned to report my findings to my temporary accountant.

"Well?' she demanded. I gave her my observations.

She took on the air of a conspirator. Leaning forward, with eyes half-closed, she moved her head slowly from side to side in a manner that suggested she was checking for eavesdroppers.

"This is what you have to do." She had lowered her voice an octave and had put her hands up to form a tunnel around her mouth, directing her words only toward me. "Just at dawn on Wednesday morning, come down to that spot. Drive down the road, leave your car at the Annie Williams Park, and walk the rest of the way. Look for the slanting birch trees so you don't get lost."

Did she think she was dealing with an amateur? I let her carry on. She must have read my mind.

"Things look different from the road than they do from the water, so pay attention, city slicker. There is a reason you need to be on the shore. When you get to the water, look down where you saw the yellow nylon rope going into the water. You know how dark the waters here are, so look closely."

As an afterthought, she added slyly, "Don't fall in."

Fall in, indeed. She was the expert at that, so I waited.

"You will see under the water two or maybe three dirty-white Styrofoam boxes tied to the rope. They are heavy; that's why they aren't bobbing up to the top."

She looked at me and waited with the expectation I would ask what was in them to weigh them down. I accommodated her. After all, it was her story, and I was meant to interject at the appropriate times as she required.

I asked, even though my experience detecting led me to believe I already knew the answer to my impending question. "So, what's in them?"

"Drr-uu-gg-ss," she said, stretching the one word out into four syllables. "But don't touch them or pull on the rope. Just look to see that they're there. They are stashed there waiting for pickup every other Wednesday, just before dawn, as soon as the ice goes out in the spring until it comes in again in the winter."

"So, I go; I look."

"Wow! Aren't you a quick study. That's what my Gramma used to say about me."

I felt like smacking that saucy grin right off her freckled face but knew the possibility of accomplishing that was less than zero.

She continued, sarcasm notwithstanding, "Just after dark, two guys will come down on foot to get the packages and two more will slide up in a rowboat. They are plan B, just in case something goes wrong with the two guys onshore not being able to get the packages. Even though they are organized, they are sloppy because they have been doing this for so long without getting caught."

She shuffled about a bit on her well-defined sitting area and continued, "Now, here's the thing: You can't do this yourself because you're not a law person. You're just a private Dick with no clout. You have to go to the OPP station and convince them this is going to happen. How you do this is your problem. Once they come down here with you, shine their lights, and catch these four guys red-handed, you will be a celebrity. Take the hero ticket as far as you want. That's up to you, and that's your payment."

This seems somewhat backward to me. She was setting me up to receive payment before she had even enlightened me of the problem she wanted me to solve for her. Was this a trick or was this just due to her age and inexperience? I was wary, of course, and waited without enquiring.

It seemed she had come to the end of her story as she reached down, picked up the diary, commenced reading, and put me on ignore. Her expression had become one of serious sadness as she flipped to a new page and appeared to be gleaning information she wished she was not privy to.

Her image was still clear, so I assumed she still had time to communicate with me before she sprinkled away. I finally broke the mood.

"Hold on a minute," I began. "How do you know so much about the drug hoist and how it works? It's not within your realm to know about such things unless you were involved somehow before your demise. You were much too young to be part of a drug ring. Next, you'll be telling me you were the leader of the gang.

"You have already established yourself as a liar and a cheat, so I think no matter what you tell me, I'll have trouble believing it anyway, but give it a shot. I'll try to read between the truth and the fairy tale."

She continued to ignore me, so I continued to badger her. "How many times have you read through your sister's diary?"

"Lost count. I should never have stolen it, let alone try to find out her secrets. All families have secrets, and they should not be told or passed on to their children. When old people say to their children, '*Oh, we don't talk about that,*' nosy children should just shut up and leave it alone. I didn't, and here I am."

"It's complicated." She sighed as she closed the diary and settled it under her bottom once more. "My sister doesn't know what happened to her diary. She just can't understand how it could have disappeared. It scares her that it is out there somewhere, and people will know what she did. She thinks all sorts of scary thoughts about it. Who has it? What will they do with it? Why did they take it? Will she be blackmailed someday? She needs to get it back and know that won't happen.

"The other thing that I don't like is that my Gramma doesn't know where I fell in the river. No one ever looked up here. If they knew about this spot where I used to hang out, it might give her some closure or something like that." She shrugged her shoulders as if she wasn't sure what closure meant but knew it was needed.

She rocked sideways with her hands under her bottom as she continued, "I want you to have her find this spot. She will know this is where I was because she has my other shoe. You will help her find the matching one that is here. She'll recognize it because she knows I had a knot tied on the laces at the last hole. They were too long, and I kept tripping over them.

"The diary will be all messed up, ripped and dirty, but that won't matter. You will find my sister's name and address inside the cover of the book, but don't go trying to read anything." She gave me a devil-dare squint.

I rubbed the back of my neck, realizing I had been stooped over in my canoe position too long with the wind blowing down and around me.

"You've left a lot of uncertainty here," I told her. "I'm to convince the OPP to come with me to catch drug smugglers pulling their merchandise out of the water. I'm to find your sister's diary and your shoe just by accident, then take the diary to her and the shoe to your Grandmother? I think I would leave myself open to investigation in both cases."

"Guess you're not as bright as you think you are then." She snorted. "Why'd you come to find me anyway?"

"I told you, I was just curious about the boats being pushed out in the river—that's all."

This kid was beyond aggravating, but now she had me corralled. "Convince me," I dared her. "Tell me what you have to keep reading that is so disturbing to you. What's the secret you were never to know and now must forever memorize? The truth may set you free." I added the last statement feeling just a little bit prophetic. It didn't work.

"Truth only sets you free when you haven't lied to get to it." She appeared to know this from experience. "You're not very organized, are you? I bet you have somebody smarter than you that keeps you on track."

I thought of my partner, Mellie, and what I sometimes put her through by jumping ahead to follow the scent of a trail. "I get by. You're getting off track on purpose. I want to hear your story, and by the looks of your fading glow, you'd better hurry."

She put the diary back in her favourite spot under her bottom and hung onto her knees once more. "My sister had a lot of books. I stole just a few. Didn't think she would miss them. She wouldn't have, but I didn't know until I made off with my snatch that I had her diary. She missed that one right away. She looked all over and was in quite a fit searching for it. How was I to know a diary is something no one else should read? Once I saw how desperate she was that someone might have it, I just had to read it.

"I stuck the other books in the loft of a boathouse downriver." She gave a sneaky grin. "Nobody knows about all the stuff I stole and hid there. Some day, somebody is in for a big surprise." Her grin turned into a giggle.

"I brought the diary here so no one could see me reading. I tumbled in right at the juicy part. I got pretty mad before that, and that's what made me slip."

"Are we going to get this story told?" I asked. "Or are you going to slip in or fade away before it even gets started?"

"Stop interrupting me then," she snapped. "I'm doing the best I can under the circumstances. I'm just a kid, ya know!"

Maybe in years but not in wisdom, I thought but didn't verbalize.

"My sister is quite a bit older than me. She's married now and has two kids. She lived not far away and would come over a lot. She was always ordering me around. Well, I found out why. She was stupid enough to write down all her true confessions and leave her diary where I could find it."

I could see her anger and resentment were not directed at her misdemeanour of stealing the diary but toward her sister for allowing her secrets to be discovered.

"Angie hung around a lot of guys when she was a teenager. Marijuana wasn't a big deal, she wrote, but of course, it just led to bigger things. I read the part where she said she delivered the drugs for the guys. Some of them got caught, but they didn't squeal on her. She thought she was home free when they were in jail, but she always talked to them and they played her along. How stupid she was, or maybe she was hooked on the stuff they gave her. They were allowed out of the two-years-less-a-day correctional prison, for baseball games, to pick up road garbage and stuff like that, and she would be right there, hanging around. That's when she started doing other stuff and writing it in her diary. See, she got pregnant and didn't know who to blame. She didn't even care. It was decided she would have the baby—that would be me.

Her mom, my Gramma, pretended to be my mom and Angie pretended to be my sister." She hesitated, then added, "Are you following me?"

I nodded in affirmation.

"No wonder I did want I wanted, stole things, and didn't care about anybody," she continued. "They lied about my life, and I don't know which criminal was my father. There was my real mother living with her other children while she kept tabs on me, and I didn't know why she was so bossy. She didn't want me living with her. She was ashamed of me and didn't want the guy she married and my sister and brother to know about me.

"It doesn't matter much now anyway. Besides, when it comes to family secrets, mine's no biggie.

"So, this diary tells me over and over again about the drug pickup just down the river a bit in the first few pages. This started before I was born. It stopped for a while; then they started it up again. Do you think I like to read about that? Angie had set up this pickup water site for them. I was in trouble before I ever took my tumble. Get busy here, will ya? Get this diary back to Angie and the shoe to Mom so I can get off this shore. Check out the drug dump and get the cops down here at the right time to make the seizure. Hurry up, get your act together, and make it happen!"

She raised one forefinger in the air and was gone with a twirl in the wind.

I had one day of rest and two workdays to consider my latest plunge into the world of my confusion. I expect I knew all along I would go through with it. I needed to figure out the best plan of attack. I convinced my reliable partner, Mellie, to cover for me if anything needing my attention arose, meanwhile I would claim a sick day for the coming Wednesday.

I drove up to my cottage Tuesday evening and was ready on foot early Wednesday morning to wander down to the clump of birch trees to see if the expected load was clipped to the yellow nylon cord and bobbing along just under the waterline. It was. I wasn't sure if this made me happy or scared. I stood for a moment, gazing out over the river, hoping to appear as a nonchalant walker enjoying the spectacular view. I then ambled back up the trail to the car park.

My next stop was the local OPP station. My credentials proved not to be impressive, even after they contacted CODA for verification. My explanation and chance discovery along the riverbank barely held up under their scrutiny. The long and the short of it ended with a willingness to send two of their finest to meet me at the car park at dusk, barring anything of more importance needed their attention. I had to settle for that.

It all went rather well, I must admit. The two constables arrived quietly on time. They accompanied me to the area of the birch trees and stood, waiting, just like they knew what they were doing. We were aware of water and boat sounds at the location in question, but nary a move was made. Before long, down the path stumbled the two landlubbers.

They were not quiet or aware of their surroundings. They made loud, rude talk with their two water rats, and that was when the official law proceeded with the roundup. All was done neatly, tidily, and without incident. I skipped the final chapter and headed straight back to Toronto to report for work the next morning.

※

I waited until early Saturday morning to once more hit the main highway heading north to Muskoka. Traffic multiplies on the weekend regardless of the time; one needs to drive as sanely as possible and go with the flow.

I was anxious to get to the grassy knoll and bush to see if the unsupervised girl with wicked ways was still rereading the diary. The car park was a beehive when I arrived. I found this a disturbing fact, as I was not aware of why. Walking down the trail, I soon realized the tale of the druggies had spread about and there were the nosey parkers who wanted to appear and identify the actual spot of the criminal activity and arrest. As they veered off to the right, I veered off to the left, where the path did not go.

She was not there. I stood back a little and looked at the riverbank. The tall uncut grass was bent slightly as it blew softly in the wind. The tangle of low-growing bushes showed no sign of human disturbance.

I stepped closer being careful, as it was quite possible to slip on the smooth grass. The angle of the bank was quite steep and ended with a metre drop. It looked quite different from this land access than from the river approach. As I bent forward to investigate the brush, I could make out downy feathers left behind as a calling card from one of last season's nesting birds. Keeping the shrubs between me and the river, for safety's sake, I squatted down and parted the scratchy branches as best I could to get a better view of what was lying among the feathers.

It was a scene for a still-life portrait of nature's use of man's objects. Caught in the V of two branches close to the ground and standing upright on its toe was one very dirty well-worn white sneaker. The tongue was turned out to form a pathway up to the inside, which was filled with dried grass and soft down. The laces had been twisted and turned upward, forming a sturdy crisscross wall. To think one small bird performed this wonder with its patience and its beak.

Just below the shoe was the diary. It was lying open with the cover on top protecting the pages. Broken branches had prevented it from falling into the river. It was not in good shape, as it appeared many little hatchlings had spent their first days on top of it learning how to live.

The scene brought forth a mental picture of the action. How upset she was to read of her birth and her mother's denial. She must have turned slightly, slamming the diary down and leaving it open at the pages she was reading. As she slipped, one foot caught in the branches, holding her suspended on her back as she flailed upside down on the bank, grasping for more support. She did say she grabbed on to some growth, but it gave way. I surmised her foot was caught securely on the branches, but as she struggled, those too-long laces came undone and her shoe slipped off, leaving her to slide right down and in, just as she described.

I continued to hold my position there in silence for a short while, not so much as a private memorial but more to do some silent thinking of how I was going to find her mother/grandmother and let her know about this place and the shoe. I also had to reunite her sister/mother with her diary. I had my payment, although the reaction of a thank-you and a handshake from the OPP for my help with the drug raid was so low-key, it hardly rated as an over-the-top, super-duper fantastically really great payment as she claimed it would be. This would not, however, be the first time a payment had fallen short of expectation.

When one is solving puzzles, it is wise to consider one piece at a time and to begin with what might be the easiest or best fit. I, therefore, decided to become knowledgeable on the case of the drowned girl. The best start would be to take my trusty laptop to the library and research the happening. The next step, I supposed, would be to approach the mother/grandmother and inform her of finding the shoe in an area that was never considered the child's point of entry. I would bring her here to see for herself and let her take the shoe if she wanted it. This would be after I removed the diary. The diary would be returned to its rightful owner with just the explanation that I found it down by the riverside. This sounded like a workable plan. I gingerly reached into the brambles with my left hand and secured the spine of the diary by placing my fingers underneath and my thumb on the top. The low growth of grass that had worked its way forward through the pages was reluctant to forfeit its hold. My hand and arm were receiving scratches from the surrounding branches that seemed to be working in conjunction with the grass.

I let it rest momentarily, then proceeded to tear away at the grass underneath that was the primary culprit reluctant to part with its treasure. I finally won the struggle. The book was opened flat and water damaged from its time in the Muskoka weather, which is not kind during the winter months. Pages were worn thin, bent, and torn. The print was faded, and I was not about to attempt to read any of it.

The shoe still hung in the crutch of the branches, not at all disturbed by my assault on the brush. I rose to my feet and backed up, holding the diary away from my person as best I could. Who knew what tiny creatures still called it home.

I returned to my car, opened the trunk, found a plastic bag, and placed the book inside, folding the bag over as best I could to keep all creatures in captivity and prevent them from invading my SUV.

Before beginning my venture, I needed to fortify myself with a Tims coffee. One was not too far out of the way—there never is. The line for the drive-up was long, as usual, so I opted to park and go inside. As I walked across the parking lot, it occurred to me I was encountering many eye contacts, smiles, head nods, and even a few "congratulations" or "good job." What was that all about?

As I stood in line in Tims, I was pointed out by a few as the guy who busted the drug ring.

"Have you seen the local paper? That is you, isn't it? Coffee on the house!"

And there on the front page of a local paper lying on the counter was yours truly backed up by Muskoka's finest, leading the druggies away, followed by a picture showing the haul that was seized.

Of course, I smiled and, as modestly as I could, accepted all compliments, answered a few questions, grabbed my coffee, and left.

So, that little brat had come through after all. I had been given my fifteen minutes of fame right there in my favourite coffee haunt. I knew I had better work at double speed if I was going to fulfill my end of the bargain.

It wasn't difficult to locate the mother/grandmother. Back copies of the local papers were on file at the library. The librarian remembered the incident and was able to direct me to the correct year and month. From there, I was able to locate the address.

My approach to the family house was announced by the baying of a floppy-eared, tail-wagging hound dog. It reminded me of my own floppy-eared Barney, who was waiting for me at the cottage. Almost immediately an elderly woman's round face appeared at the half window of the door. I smiled as friendly as I could and waited. She gave a nod and opened the door. She was a large woman, and her being filled the doorway. She held on to the door jamb as if she needed the support.

"I recognize you from the paper," she began at once. "What brings you here? I know nothing about the men or the drugs you found. Is anyone I know involved? Have you any more information?"

Although I was not expecting a welcome of this sort, I recognized the forthcoming questioning as something that seemed to run in the family.

"I don't mean to intrude on your business and sorrow, ma'am, but while I was down by the river, I spotted something that may be of interest to you."

She moved her head slightly to the left, with only her eyes showing an interest.

I continued, "I understand at the time of your daughter's accidental drowning, the searchers were unable to locate where she had gone into the river. If you are still wondering about that, I think I may be able to assist you in finding the answer."

She took a deep breath and exhaled just as deeply. "I'd like that," she finally whispered.

"If you could come with me, I've something I'd like to show you." I spoke as tenderly as I could, realizing I was no doubt bringing forth unwanted memories. "If now is not a good time, let me know when would suit you."

She raised her stature and gave a steady answer. "Now would be just as good as any time, sir," she declared.

I waited on the doorstep while she retreated to change into her walking shoes and locate her purse. She appeared within five minutes and announced, "Well, let's be off to wherever it is you think I should be going." She chuckled under her breath.

She remained silent as I drove to the Annie Williams parking area. When we arrived, she looked around in recognition. "I haven't been here in quite a while, but it looks just the same. The trees are a little bigger; that's all."

She waited until I went around, opened the door and helped her out. I had moved the seat back as far as it would go, but with her bulk, her movements were slow. It was not hard to recognize the symptoms of arthritis either. She nodded her head to give her thanks.

I led her carefully down the path to the brush, staying slightly ahead and to the side of her so she could reach my arm in case she needed extra support. She did not query as to why or where I was taking her. I found that slightly odd, as I thought there would be at least a few items she would need to clarify before putting her trust in the word of a stranger, let alone allowing him to take her out into a deserted field by the river. Had my reputation been that golden?

As we approached the bush, I stopped and bent down as I had before, parting the bushes to reveal the hanging shoe.

I heard her gasp and utter, "Oh my! It's Becc's other shoe! How did you find it? How did you know it was here? How did you know it was hers? Is this where she fell in? Oh my!"

She made a sudden lurch forward, and it was all I could do to stand up and hold her back to prevent her from sliding in as Becc had done. She had more than a few pounds on me, so this was not an easy task. I had visions of us both floundering forth.

"Stay back," I ordered. "The grass is slippery. I'll get it for you."

Much to my relief, she did just that, all the while keeping her eyes on the bush as if the shoe might vanish if she blinked.

Once I was sure she was back far enough on level ground, I once more approached the bush and crouched. Ignoring the scratching of the smaller branches that were reluctant to give up their hold on the object they had entwined so securely, I pulled it toward me slowly. The long laces were covered with nettles and downy fluff. I turned it upside down, checking for little inhabitants before presenting it to Becc's grandmother.

I turned and walked the few steps back to her. Holding the shoe in both hands, I held it forth to her. She looked at it for a moment with a restful look on her wrinkled face.

"She must have slipped right in," she said. "Her foot was caught, wasn't it? She must have been so scared. It was an accident, wasn't it? She was by herself, wasn't she?" She took the shoe and held it to her bosom. As she turned, I heard her whisper, "She was always by herself, poor baby."

We walked back to the car in silence, and the silence prevailed as I drove her back to her home. She struggled out of the car on her own without waiting for my help. She was still holding the shoe tightly in her hand.

She gave me no word of thanks or recognition as she proceeded to her front door and disappeared inside. I made a U-turn and headed back to the car park to sit for a moment in solitude.

My GPS took me east along Taylor Road and a few kilometres out of town. Angie's house was situated on a hill at the end of a long curved driveway, banked on either side by tall maples. *Hope husband has a snowplough*, I mused as I slowly wended my way forth.

Jumping barking dogs announced my arrival before I came to a full stop in front of an open-door garage that sported a 5.4M Princecraft fishing boat. A woman I assumed was Angie ambled out of the garage, wiping her hands on an oil rag. She ignored the dogs, and they ignored her. I ignored them as well and stayed right where I was; they were Dobermans. As she approached my SUV, I opened the window. She bent down slightly and asked, "Can I help you?" She showed no recognition for my recent fame.

"I may have something that belongs to you." I had learned to jump right into the reason for me being there, as this family seemed to prefer that. "I found it when I was walking by the Muskoka River. It looks like it had been there for quite a while. I looked up the name that was on the inside cover, and it led me to you. It's in a plastic bag in the hatch. Take a look. If it's yours, please take it. If it's not yours, well, just leave it be."

I popped the hatch and waited.

She backed up. Wordlessly, she moved around to the back of my vehicle with the three Dobermans moving with her. I watched through my mirror as best I could as she leaned forward and brought the bag closer to her. It seemed she immediately identified its contents because her face took on a look of horrified recognition. She picked the bag up in both hands and walked around to me.

She stood back from me and announced, "It's mine! Thanks for bringing it." She waved me off and headed back into the garage.

Very well, my debt was paid, and this family had been stranger than strange. I was now through with them. Keeping that thought to myself, once more, I made a U-turn and headed back to my cottage and Barney for the rest of the weekend.

I arrived at the CODA office well rested and full of vim and vigour Monday morning, only to be greeted by Mellie giving me a heads-up and a warning.

"Your appearance is requested in the upper office ASAP. I think it has to do with your 'sick day' last week."

The giver of assignments was wearing a quizzical face as I entered his domain. He pointed to a copy of the local Bracebridge paper sporting my photo and the drug bust write-up.

"Are you moonlighting on sick leave, O'Patrick? Do you know what sick leave is for? Would you be interested in another type of leave? Are you looking for employment with the OPP? Can you explain this to me? Make me understand how this came about. I'll wait."

And I thought the strange family had questions. I knew I had to give him a once-upon-a-time explanation, as he would never understand my aura dilemma.

Even Mellie did not.

"Well, sir," I began, "This is the way of it...."

10 EMERALDS FROM THE ISLE

ON A MISSION TO visit as many parks as our fair city has to offer, I took the time one sunny Sunday, a little while back in my life, to take Barney for a walk along the pathways of High Park. After enough exercise for both of us, I found and captured an empty bench. There I sat relaxed while Barney flopped at my feet, head on paws and eyes threatening to close. Suddenly, I became aware of a draft of cold air to the right of me. That should not be happening on a warm, sunny day, which was my first clue that I should not have allowed my mind to flow freely. I could not resist turning my head toward the source of this draft, of course, and there he was, sitting beside me and happily feeding ghostly pigeons that only we could see.

He was a smiling, friendly-looking old chap with a twitching moustache. He was dressed quite comfortably in a tweed sports jacket and dark slacks. The collar of his white shirt was open; he carried his neck wrinkles with no shame.

Someone's old grandpa, I surmised. No harm here, just a brief "No, go away; I'm not interested" and he would get the hint.

I should have known he was from the generation of the more determined. I waited. So did he. *Okay, you win*: I spoke first. No one was within earshot at that moment to think I was carrying on a monologue. It doesn't matter much these days anyway, as we see and ignore many people talking into invisible earpieces and laughing out loud all by themselves. I had learned by now to keep my hand movements to a minimum, as that attracted more queries about my mental state than my vocalization.

"Are you a ghost or a spirit?" I questioned.

"A ghost," he replied without breaking his motion of feeding the invisible pigeons with invisible seeds. "If I were a spirit, I would have to stay within the boundaries of my demise, and, young man, I didn't expire on this park bench, and I would have the ability to move things and solve my dilemma, but as a ghost, I can only bounce myself about, but you are aware of that." He carefully used the back of his hand to dust ghost birdseed residue off the front of his white shirt. "Ah, it was such a delight to feed the birds in this park with my Maggie in the old days. We used this bench quite a bit. I'm so glad to have caught you here. You don't come by here often."

Not short on words, this old fellow. Long-winded, or perhaps he hadn't had a chance to bend a human ear for a while. I waited in silence.

He tuned up and began to sing a Broadway tune that would have been popular in his heyday. "*Feed the birds, a tuppence a bag, tuppence, tuppence . . .*" he sang.

"You have a request, I gather?" I interrupted him, as I was afraid his song might erupt into a soft shoe dance routine at any moment. "Has it something to do with your Maggie? Your wife, perhaps?" I knew I was hooked. He wouldn't even have to try to convince me. I'm a sucker for love that has lasted through the tides of time.

He stopped singing, folded over the top of his birdseed bag, and placed it to the side of him. He crossed his skinny legs, clasped his hands in front of him, and turned to me with a grandfatherly smile. "Only in a roundabout way," he commenced. "So, please listen with a little patience while I tell you my tale. It has to do with my granddaughter, Shauna, and an exquisite family bracelet my Maggie, her grandmother, had left her, but she doesn't have it." He bowed his head in sadness.

I raised one hand, palm facing him. "Before you go any further, sir, I can only assume you have been in contact with some of my other ghost clients and are aware there's a payment for my services. What payment can you give me?"

He contemplated, hands still clasped, wiggled that handlebar moustache with a twitch, and then seemly satisfied with his decision, gave me a knowing smile and declared quite emphatically, "I can tell you the family secret you have been yearning to know most of your life. You thought it was your mother that kept it from you, but no. Your mother didn't have the information. It was your dearly departed grandmother that kept the secret."

Now that piece of information left me so startled, I remained slack-jawed and speechless.

So, he continued. "I met her briefly as she passed over. She didn't need to stick around here, you understand. She held no regrets or wishes left undone in her life, but you see, she saw no need to pass the secret on. Those of us who are descendants from a certain Irish area recognize and feel free to confide and help each other when deemed necessary. I believe that is why she took time to bide awhile and discuss the matter before she travelled on. She told me of the weakness in your aura and bid me welcome to use it if I felt the need. Well, my lad, I feel the need, and in return, I shall tell you what your dear granny said. It is the story of how you came to have a weak link in your aura."

He rolled his thumbs around each other as he bounced one foot up and down at the end of his crossed legs. He looked so self-satisfied.

Although I was punched, I was trying to do some up-ahead thinking. Naturally, I had been wanting to understand why I have a curse upon my aura, but what would be the ripple effects of this discovery? Everything has a cause and effect, but I knew I would have to take the chance. How could a mere mortal refuse a mind-bending offer such as that?

"A done deal!" I agreed eagerly, even before I had the details of his request. We couldn't seal the agreement with a handshake, as I knew I would grasp nothing but a handful of chilly air.

He settled back in a comfortable ghostly manner, unclasped his hands, wrapped them around his waist, and leaned in closer, invading my space. Why do they always do that to me? It causes uncomfortable icy drafts. I think they enjoy my reaction.

"It won't take you long to unravel what is ravelled," he said with a knowing chuckle. When ghosts play their "I know something you don't know" game, it makes me grit my teeth; it sets me back several places on the game board. Spirits don't play these mind games. They are much more opinionated and ruder. They prefer to take the lead by telling me what to do.

"Fill me in," I conceded. "Continue with the telling of your tale."

"I don't have much to fill, I'm afraid. The bracelet does have value on the monetary market but has greater value in the family story. You see"—he cocked his head over my way just a tad too close for my liking, making me realize the old fellow must have lost his hearing aid in the crossing—"Granddaughter Shauna is the seventh generation in the maternal line coming down through my darling Maggie. That takes us all the way back to the Great Potato Famine in the dear old Emerald Isle."

The temptation to interrupt and get on with what he wanted was itching me, but as I turned to look at this thin face with melancholy eyes, it was as plain as the white on a ghost that this gentleman was down a memory lane that was not to be stopped until he was ready.

He wiggled about a bit on his boney bottom as he shifted into high gear. "As the story is told, a Baron in the County Tipperary twinkled his eye on Aoife"—that sounds like Eva to us—"and while she was in service at his castle, lighting the fires, polishing the silver, and tending to all the jobs that were done by the serving class, she was also doomed to service the Baron as well. Thus, her darling daughter, Roisin"—that sounds like ro-sheen to us—"arrived on the scene. Now the Baron, with a castle full of sons, took an affection to Roisin, but of course, she was born on the wrong side of the blanket, wasn't she? He scribed from his inkhorn into his family book, much to the chagrin of his wife, '*Roisin McMurray, bastard daughter of the Baron*' with Aoife's name and date. He then presented Aoife with a gold bracelet with an intricate filigree-woven design of tiny harps and hounds depicting the family crest and holding a smattering of the Isle's green emeralds. The clasp was doubled with a fine gold chain to secure it in case of breakage. He instructed her to keep it in safekeeping for Roisin, as she and her descendants would forever be under the protection of the vast influence of the Baron. Roisin was to wear it on her wedding day and give it to her firstborn daughter on her wedding day and hand it down through the generations to come."

He rolled one hand to indicate how fast those generations had flown by. "It went well for all these years until now."

It was a fascinating tale. I was caught up in the telling to the point that it took me a moment to realize his speech was fading and there was no longer a cold draft coming from his direction. He was fading fast.

"I've used up my power supply." He wheezed. "I'll find you when I've rejuvenated once more. Check out the family, starting with Maggie's sister, Dorothy Webb. She coveted that bracelet, but she didn't have any girls, just two lame-brained sons."

"That's all you got? Give me dates, names, places, the country even. Are we still in Ireland?" A soft, warm breeze lofted by my face, so I knew he was gone.

I leaned back, feeling more exhausted than I realized. What an interesting mystery to unravel. I thought about the few clues I had. If he and Maggie sat upon this very bench, I would start with the assumption they walked to the park, so they must have lived close by. High Park south of Bloor Street West is a favourite spot for westside Torontonians, due to its versatility and harmony. I fantasized they even entertained a young Shauna with a visit to the zoo and then a picnic. But here I was, wool-gathering much like the old gentleman. I didn't even get his name.

I gathered up my scanty clues and placed them together in an uncompleted memory box to mull over. I had the west end of the city, deceased grandmother Maggie, no last name, her sister, Dorothy Webb, with two sons, granddaughter Shauna, surname unknown, a grand description of the bracelet, whereabouts unknown, and prime suspect, Dorothy Webb.

Judging by the mannerisms and clothing of this fellow, I surmised he would have been interred a few years ago. He was well-spoken in an educated manner; his clothes appeared neat, clean, and comfortable. When he crossed his legs, I noted the good quality of his slacks and black laced shoes, ergo he had lived in middle or upper-middle-class comfort.

CODA had no work for me at that time, and this ghostly case was calling with the promised payment of enlightening me as to why I have a weak link in my aura. Following clues and instinct is not difficult these days, as with the click of a mouse or the slide of a finger, everyone knows everyone's business.

I toed Barney on his belly. "C'mon Barn, time to move."

We exited the park by the Bloor Street entrance and boarded the first streetcar heading east. Dogs are allowed if they are small and you can hang on to them, and Barney understands he must be on his best behaviour when aboard. This is the best mode of transportation in our city of trees.

Once in the confines of my corner of the world, I googled Dorothy Webb. Quite a surprise, it was, to discover how many Dorothy Webbs are out there and how many have made their home in my city. There were ads for agencies willing to do searches for you, including my employer. Undaunted, I checked out the Dorothys, starting at the top and eliminating many quickly. My Dorothy would be elderly, with sons and perhaps grandsons with the Webb name. Over to Facebook, I slid, searching for the name within the confines of Ontario. So many people pose with pictures of their family, pets, homes, and many other aspects of their private lives. A lot to scroll and rather boring, but perhaps more productive than Google.

With a beer to the right of my laptop and a sub to the left, it took the better part of the evening before—*voila!*—there they were! The brothers Webb! Their page sported a backyard picture of them with their arms over each other's shoulders as they stood behind a white wooden lawn chair that held a portly elderly lady, who could be none other than their mother, Dorothy. All smiles, they were, as families should be. I scrolled down through the posted pictures and discovered their backyard kiddy pool, kiddies, and wives as well. Winter photos showed snowball fights and families dressed in beautiful Irish cable-knit sweaters, hats, and gloves. Ten years of photos and comments showed the growth of the loves and losses of their family. All were there to see. One big happy family, very normal and ho-hum as most families are. People post their lives on these open sites and then are outraged when hacked.

Their postings gave me all I needed to know. The Christmas family dinner from a few years ago showed all with smiling faces and hugs. Comments and replies under the posted pictures told me which young lady was cousin Shauna West and who were her parents. There in a family group, well in the background, stood their Great Uncle Nelson and their Great Aunt too. I recognized my ghostly employer because of his white shirt and moustache.

I shut down the Webb family and did some clicking to search for Miss Shauna West. She, too, being Miss Modern, had also borne her soul online. She was very much a young beauty. The Irish shone through. Perhaps I am a little biased, but the auburn hair and green eyes could only have been handed down through seven generations from across the Irish Sea. Her FB page showed me an invitation to her engagement party and many happy groupings from her wedding day. Her flowing bridal dress and devoted husband at her side made a perfect picture, except there was no gold emerald bracelet shining on her right wrist. Was the need for the baron's protection merely a myth by now? Regardless!

May the Irish saints preserve us! This lovely child should have what was rightfully hers!

"So, then, Grandpa Nelson, let's find it!" I chided myself immediately for shouting out like that, as the very act could bring forth unwanted company when alone.

A little more digging revealed the facts I needed. Shauna's mother had died too soon. She had not been able to present Shauna with this generational treasure. This must have weighed heavily on Grandma Nelson's mind and why she and then her devoted husband were so persistent that the bracelet should be with Shauna.

I decided to present myself at Shauna West-Best's place of abode. Coward that I can be at times, I chose a Saturday when I was privy to the fact that her husband was out golfing for the day. I needed to be sure that the bracelet was mentioned in her grandmother's will and that Shauna was meant to have it. As always, stick to the truth as much as possible.

~~~

I dressed appropriately in my second-best navy blue suit and matching tie, sporting tiny Maple Leaf logos. I knocked politely as I stood in front of the Best's front door. Shauna answered quickly as if she had observed my approach. With the screen door between us, locked, she asked defensively, "Yes?" One cannot be too careful in the city these days.

"Shauna West-Best?" I asked quite formally.

"Yes?" she answered just as formally.

"So sorry to bother you. My name is Daniel O'Patrick. I'm from an investigation agency following up on the bequests in your grandmother Nelson's will." I attempted to hand her one of my cards, but of course, the screen door prevented this.

Shauna hesitated briefly, then unlatched the door. She opened it slightly to receive my card. I was crossing my fingers it would not receive too much scrutiny or invite a phone call for verification.

After a cursory glance at it, Shauna looked up at me and gave me her confession. "There are one or two items not accounted for, I'm afraid. I still have a few pieces of her furniture that I haven't let my uncles know about. They're here in my house."

Such an honest child. "Is that all then?" I coached.

"Well, no. There is an heirloom bracelet that can't be found. Grandma always kept it locked in her treasure chest." Shauna laughed. "It's not really a treasure chest. It's a little jewellery box from long ago. Grandma told me her mother gave it to her one Christmas when she was a little girl. It was always special to her. I have it now, and I treasure it. That's why I call it a treasure chest. It's the kind, you know, when you opened the lid, up pops tiny plastic birds flying in a circle and tweeting a tune from *My Fair Lady*. 'Feed the Birds,' it's called." Shauna used her hands to indicate how the tiny birds on a wire would perform their stunt.

"Grandma always kept the box locked. The tiny key was taped to the bottom of the box. When she would show me the bracelet, she would make a ritual of unlocking the box, taking the bracelet out, and holding it just so. Then she would put it on my wrist for us to admire before returning it to her box and locking it up again. It was a flimsy lock, but it always opened. When I was given Grandma's jewellery box, it wasn't locked. The key was gone, and her bracelet was nowhere to be found." Shauna looked very sad after finishing her tale of woe.

I gave her a moment of silence, then asked as sorrowfully as I could, "Do you have a copy of her will?"

When she gave an affirmative nod, I broached the next hurdle. "Would you permit me to have a look at it?" Experience had taught me not to be the one to initiate an invite into the house.

"Yes, of course," she responded. "Wait a moment, I'll get it."

So careful, she was. She had not invited me, a stranger, into her home when she was alone. I perched on the small bench that was to the side of the door and waited. She returned momentarily and came out. She handed me a tri-folded, three-page document. It didn't take me long to confirm the old man's story.

Item number five: *"The Emerald Isle bracelet that I received from my mother, Elise O'Connell, is to be given into the care of Shauna West when she marries as it continues through the maternal side of our family to females only. If there are no females to hand it down to, it is to be donated to the museum in Tipperary, along with its history."*

"You still have the jewellery box?"

"Yes."

"May I see it?"

"Why?"

"I would like to ascertain if the lock was broken or opened with the key. Are there scrape marks on it? Where could the key be? Who knew the bracelet was there? You see, I am a detective, Mrs. West-Best. I am doing my best to detect."

After a slight hesitation, she lifted the latch, opened the door, and waved me through.

Her house was a typical three-bedroom bungalow one would expect for a young couple just beginning this chapter of their lives. When Shauna disappeared down the hall to retrieve the box, I visually checked out her living room for furniture quality and display—an old habit instilled in us detectives. Situated over the back of her sofa was a colourful hand-knit afghan. The design was complicated. Coming from a family with sisters who knit, I recognized the cable and basketweave stitches.

"Shauna," I said when she returned. "What a lovely throw; did you knit that?"

"No," she scoffed. "I'm not that clever. My great aunt Dorothy is a compulsive knitter. She keeps us all cozy and warm with her knitting expertise, whether we want it or not. She knits on consignment and sells her items at crafts shows as well. Here's the treasure box. Have a look."

The box was beige, with a faux quilted plastic cover. Shades of the fifties by the age of it. The inside was completely lined with crimson silk. When I lifted the lid, up rose a shelf on side hinges. Under the lid was a small mirror. A trio of white birds twirled about, the mirror making them look like a large flock as the wound-up mechanism burst forth the aforesaid tune. This jewellery-music box had been given tender loving care over the years. No damage was done when opening it. No key was with it.

I carefully closed the lid, trapping the birds inside once more, and handed it back to Shauna. I thanked her for her time and asked her for her great aunt's address. I assured her there would be a follow-up, but when, I did not know. I was in good spirits when I left her.

After a little more online research, I found great aunt Dorothy's web page heralding her stock of knitted items for sale or any knitted item you fancied could be taken on consignment. I spent a couple of days browsing through local thrift shops and Sally Ann stores until I found my show-and-tell. My call to the great aunt went as follows.

"Hello, Mrs. Webb, you don't know me, but I was visiting with Shauna last week." *Stick as close to the truth as possible.* "She has a beautiful afghan on her couch. She told me you made it for her. You do a wonderful job."

"Oh, thank you." She was proud of her work. "Is there something I can knit for you?"

"I hope so. I have an old knitted afghan in very bad shape. It can't be salvaged, I'm afraid. Would it be possible for you to knit a new one in the same size and colour, using the same stitches?"

"I would have to see it. Can you email me some pictures?"

"It might be better if you saw the real thing, as the pattern varies throughout. Could I drop it off at your convenience? Cost is of no consequence, but time is."

After a brief hesitation, I think the jingle of loonies and toonies danced in her head, as she responded, "I am at my craft show most weekends but home during the weekdays. What would suit you best?"

"Any weekday is fine for me," I assured her. "I am north at my cottage most weekends."

"Tomorrow, then? At two o'clock? Can I text you the directions at this number?"

"Perfect," I purred.

Keeping my time in mind, I googled her address and drove to Markham on the outskirts of the city. I had no trouble finding the twisting drive leading up to Dorothy's high rise. Carrying my tattered and torn Sally Ann afghan in a green garbage bag, but with TLC, I entered her building's lobby and pushed the button for her condo. She promptly answered, confirmed my identity, and allowed me entry. I was whisked away in a speedy elevator up to the twelfth floor. Dorothy was out in the hall ready to direct me into her cliff dwelling.

Dorothy's living space was uncomfortably warm and stuffy. It was cluttered with books, magazines, swatches of material, and a sewing machine. It was overloaded with balls and hanks of wool in every colour, shape, and size. Rays of sunlight slanted through the closed windows and a slight waft of air showed a flutter of thread tufts floating willy-nilly around the room—an asthma sufferer's nightmare. Several articles on knitting needles in various stages of completion were haphazardly placed around the room. At one end of the overstuffed sofa was a clearing where it appeared Dorothy sat during her knitting time. There was a footstool for her feet, a tall lamp for her eyes, and, close to the window, a birdcage held one tiny bird.

The whole scene overwhelmed me and left me nearly speechless. Why the first thing out of my mouth was, "Oh, you have a canary!" I don't know.

Dorothy looked rather insulted. "No," she answered. "Eva is a parakeet."

Right on cue, this little bird began to sing. Just three notes, she sang. "*Dohhhhh, me, soh . . . Dohhhhh, me, soh.*"

I proceeded to take my afghan out of the green bag and presented it to Dorothy. She inspected it carefully, taking in every detail. I could tell she was indeed a master at her trade. She looked at the type of stitches and their placement. She thought she had a couple of knitting books with patterns much like these. It was an old pattern, she explained as she pointed to each eight-by-eight-inch square block while she named the stitches. A cable here, a basket weave there; here a shell, there a wave, everywhere a buttonhole knave. All the while we were exchanging knitting knots, the little parakeet never stopped her song. Dorothy finally noticed my distraction.

"Don't mind, Eva," she said. "Typical of her lineage, she only sings one tune and it goes on and on. I don't even hear it anymore. She is pretty, though, don't you think?"

I nodded in agreement, wondering all the while what I had gotten myself into and how I was going to extract myself from this overly heated woollen mill without passing out and having nothing to show for it except an order for an unwanted afghan.

"I have all my patterns on file in my second bedroom office desk. I'll go and have a look." Dorothy placed my afghan under one arm, holding it with her elbow, and waddled over to a sideboard. She removed the head lid off a ceramic cookie jar in the shape of a cheeky red-breasted robin and dipped her hand in; it came back out as a fist holding birdseed.

"Here." She beckoned me over. "Hold this in your hand and make friends with Eva while I am looking for your pattern. She takes kindly to young gentlemen."

I did her bidding, neither of us paying the least bit of attention to the escaping seeds that landed on the wool-fluffed floor. She replaced the robin's head with a clatter, then lumbered her way across the room, a short distance actually, and released the clasp on the tiny door of Eva's cage. Eva wasted no time escaping and flying high in circles around the room. It was obvious this was a ritual for her.

"Give her a moment; then hold your hand out," Dorothy commanded as she once more laboured across her living room, down her hall, and out of sight.

I watched Eva flit about in freedom from her cage. Up near the ceiling, she flew, then swooped down and around in carousel motion. I slowly uncurled my fingers and waited for her landing. Eva made a graceful approach, stuttering in mid-air with wings back. Her tiny feet barely grazed my hand when she pecked at the seeds and flew off once more. She glided across the room diagonally, took a dive, and I lost sight of her.

Not good! I knew if I lost Eva, I'd lose my life. A few strides took me across the room, and looking down into a dark corner, in the shadow of an armchair and an end table, I spied Eva perched on top of balls of yarns that were captured in a wicker basket. If not for Eva's bright colouring and quick movements against the drab green of the yarn, I would have missed her. She dug and was almost buried under the top ball as she pecked at the yarn in the middle.

I bent over the arm of the chair and reached around the end table, hoping to catch her before she became completely tangled in wool. To be on the safe side, I lifted not only Eva but the ball she was bent on attacking. One must be gentle when holding a small bird, so I held the ball of green yarn instead. She seemed quite content to perch on top and peck away as if she was nest building. It was then I spied a glint of gold as she attacked the wool. Keeping the ball and Eva in one hand, I carefully tried to separate the strands of yarn with the fingers of the other. Not an easy task, as Eva was still on the attack. It could not have been possible, but it appeared that she gave me a knowing bird's eye look before she stopped her attack and allowed me to pull out the glittering object. Yes, indeed, it was a delicate gold filigree bracelet with sparkling emeralds set on tiny harps and hounds. Off Eva flew across the room, and she perched on the lid of the cookie jar. She warbled her three notes and was quite aware of where her reward should come from.

I wasn't above taking, as the bracelet had already been taken. I slipped it into my inside jacket pocket, closed up the hole in the yarn ball, and replaced it as carefully as I could to its original position—just in time, I might add, as I heard Dorothy thumping down the hall toward the room. I assumed a nonchalant stance near the cookie jar and tried to match Eva's three notes with a whistle. Dorothy entered the room, brandishing a magazine on the top of my afghan.

"I think I have just the pattern for you." She was quite pleased with herself as she put the afghan down on the sideboard and showed me a picture and pattern of a colourful, crazy quilt throw.

"Oh, exactly!" I gushed in joy. "You really are a wonder, Mrs. Webb. I will leave this with you." I patted the top of my Sally Ann rescue. I'll check in with you in a month or so. Is that enough time? Here's a down payment for the materials and your work."

I had no idea of the cost, so I peeled off three fifties and laid them on top of my tattered and torn accomplice.

As I headed out the door, I heard Dorothy calling, "Your name? How can I get in touch with you?"

───

Shauna was ecstatic when I presented her with her bracelet. Ask no questions, I made her promise before I turned it over. Then I faded away into the sunset, never to see her again but to wait in anticipation for my payment.

It was all I could do to hold off for two weeks before taking Barney on another walk along the High Park trail and ending up at grandfather's favourite bench, thinking perhaps he may be more comfortable there. I was not disappointed. As sure as ghosts can glide, he appeared before long. I found it interesting no pigeons visited us this time.

Finally, the old man spoke. I had outwaited him.

"Your grandmother—on your mother's side, that is—loved you dearly and watched over you as best she could. She and your mother, too, were watching to see if you were receiving signals from visitors from another realm. I am not privy to how soon in your life some found their way through your aura, but according to your grandmother, you rejected them when you entered your teen years. They were interfering with your social life, so you brushed them off as annoying instances. They soon gave up and left.

"But, my lad, your curiosity got the best of you and you acknowledged there was something or someone there that needed to be identified. Unwittingly, you invited them in through the weak link and that opened up the way for others."

"I know that," I interjected. "Get to the telling of why before you run out of energy. I've been left in the lurch before."

He gave me a look of disdain and continued, "It is a condition handed down from your grandmother's mother; that would be your great-grandmother. She was born into the roving life of the Irish gypsies. Call them gypsies, tinkers or travellers, they all were the rovers across the Isle. The men were all tall, dark, and handsome lads and had little trouble winning the hearts of maidens as they passed through their villages. So it was with your two-times great. She followed her Gypsy rover and gave birth to her daughter in his rolling caravan. The travelling group would set up camp outside villages and towns and take part in the local entertainment.

"It is always difficult to determine what is fact and what is folklore from the stories handed down. Ireland is on top of the heap for having many mystical folklore that has taken root in belief. There are the fairies, leprechauns, rainbow gold, and banshees. Your mysterious tall dark tinker ancestor had a touch of what some call the third eye. Yes, he could see the restless ghosts and spirits of those that had gone on. He used this power to elaborate and spin an Irish tale for any villager who wished to contact a recently departed— as long as they crossed his palm with silver, of course. The stories he related to them often ended with a dangling thread that enticed the customer to return with more silver to discover more about their past or their future.

"While your Gypsy great-great-grandfather used his ability as often as he could with worried clients, it came to pass that the edge of his aura or his senses beyond our understanding became weakened and he found old souls were sneaking in and asking for favours. He thrived on the payments, as this fed his family during the time of Ireland's darkest years.

"As his years rolled on and his fortunes improved, he tired of the game. That was what it was to him. He was not in the occupation of helping others. He found a way to close the gap, but I am not sure it will work for you, Daniel. You like to help, and you have the downfall of curiosity."

"So, what did he do?"

He paused, and as I saw him sparkle, it was obvious he had little time left with me. "Think back to what you did when they started to interfere with your young and foolish love affairs. You've had the wherewithal to stop them all along, but deep down, you must admit, you are so curious about them and loved the surprise payments—admit it now. So, stop it if you want or carry on. It is entirely up to you.

"There, you have my payment, my boy. Be careful what you wish for. Go pick up your afghan." He couldn't keep the laughter out of his voice. "Unlike you, dear Dorothy does deal in cash, and you owe her much more." And with a swoosh of frigid air, he was gone.

So, that was it! I had this weak link in my aura because of a wandering Gypsy ancestor. Wasn't it enough I had inherited blue eyes and a congenial personality? Was there a way to close this link much like when Wendy sewed up Peter Pan's shadow when it became loose?

Shauna's grandfather did say I had stopped them from coming through when I was young and foolish. What was it that I did or didn't do?

I stood up and gave a tug on Barney's leash. He was more than ready to waddle forth. We took the path meandering down along Wendigo Pond. We stopped to admire the view. A family of mallards was marching in unison along the bank.

A sudden drift of iciness moved along my left side. I recognized it for what it was. No, I didn't want to know. No, I mustn't be curious.

I turned to my right and walked away. The warmer air found me.

Was that all I had to do? Was it really that easy? I had to ignore, turn away and not look. Maybe I could take a sneaky peek back to see who was. . . .

Barney pulled me ahead, just in time.

ACKNOWLEDGMENTS

MY FRIEND PATRICIA HAGER, from North Dakota, formed the Destin Florida Snowbird Writers Group in 2017. The writers in this group were from all over the USA and Canada. They were very supportive and encouraging while I was running my ideas by them. They laughed in the right places and came up with scenarios for Detective Daniel O'Patrick. (He didn't have a name then.)

During the COVID-19 pandemic, we met by Zoom, and we still do. Patricia showed me her old battered trumpet and later a picture of her standing in a river. The bushes behind her looked like a little mischievous girl, knees up, reading a book and laughing. My imagination took over.

In my opinion, Wynton Marsalis, playing his trumpet, is at the top of the class. You can catch him on YouTube playing "Amazing Grace" in the Federal Hall and joining the Treme Brass Band in a funeral march in New Orleans.

Although a book of fiction, unfortunately, the story of Stringbean Akeman and his wife, Estelle, is true.

I am a first-generation Canadian, raised on stories from Ireland and Scotland. Each time a family story was told, it took a different twist at the end. My maternal grandfather worked on the Titanic as a Joiner. Different stories were told about that.

Many things in Daniel's tellings are interactions and incidences from my past, some from long ago meeting up with the present. I still have my golf hole-in-one trophy from 2004, but I have no idea where Barney came from.

Printed in Canada